A
Harlequin
Romance

OTHER

Harlequin Romances

by MARY BURCHELL

JUST A NICE GIRL

by

MARY BURCHELL

HARLEQUIN BOOKS   TORONTO
WINNIPEG

Harlequin edition published October 1975

SBN 373-01919-X

Original hard cover edition published
by Mills & Boon Limited.

*All the characters in this book have no existence outside the
imagination of the Author, and have no relation whatsoever to
anyone bearing the same name or names. They are not even
distantly inspired by any individual known or unknown to the
Author, and all the incidents are pure invention.*

The Harlequin trade mark, consisting of the word
HARLEQUIN and the portrayal of a Harlequin, is registered
in the United States Patent Office and in the Canada Trade
Marks Office.

Printed in Canada

1919

CHAPTER I

"It isn't even," Aunt Katherine was saying, "as though Nicola were exceptionally pretty. She could be as stupid as my Diana, for instance, without it mattering, so long as she *looked* like Diana. But she doesn't."

Aunt Katherine was not vexed about it. She was not even plaintive, because that was not her way. She was simply voicing a regrettable truth with absolute finality. And Nicola felt correspondingly depressed by it.

She knew she had not been meant to hear the remark. —that she was, in fact, only demonstrating once more the truth of the saying that eavesdroppers must not expect to hear anything good of themselves. But then she had not intended to eavesdrop. It was only that Aunt Katherine's clear, positive tones were apt to carry a little farther than she meant them to.

As it was, Nicola had to listen very carefully (which she shamelessly did) in order to catch old Miss Pottington's reply.

"Dear Mrs. Round"—Miss Pottington often prefaced whatever she was going to say in this manner, giving one the impression that she was reading a letter aloud—"Dear Mrs. Round, you must remember that having four such *exceptional* daughters yourself, you probably expect a very high standard."

"Yes, I dare say," agreed Aunt Katherine. "But then that makes it all the more marked. She's so extremely mediocre when she is measured up against my girls."

5

"Dear Mrs. Round"—Miss Pottington laughed protestingly—"the geese can't all be swans. After all, there is nothing *wrong* with Nicola. She is what you might call just a nice, ordinary girl."

"Oh, she is a *nice* girl, poor child," agreed Aunt Katherine, in a tone that would have deterred anyone from wishing to know any more about her.

And at that point Nicola slipped away, taking with her the vague impression that even to be a homicidal lunatic would at any rate be more interesting and remarkable than to be just what she was—a nice girl, poor child.

She went out of the house by the side-door, into the long kitchen garden that stretched down to the wood-sheds at the boundary of her aunt's ground. Usually these were deserted in the middle of the afternoon, and they seemed very attractive in prospect to Nicola for that very reason.

But as she neared the larger shed—empty, as yet, of the piles of clean-smelling logs that would accumulate there during the late summer and early autumn—she heard sounds of unmistakable activity within, and the slightly hoarse, entirely unmusical humming which accompanied the sounds told her that the youngest cousin, Edward, was there on some mysterious business of his own.

Nicola pushed open the top half of the door, and leant her arms on the lower half, to look into the cool, pleasant interior of the big wood shed, where a stocky little boy of twelve sawed away earnestly at some pieces of wood.

"Hallo, Edward. What are you doing?"

"Working."

6

"Yes, I know. But what are you working *at*?"

"Making a toy car for the Fraser kid."

"Are you really? That's pretty difficult, isn't it? May I come in and watch you?"

"If you won't get in the way."

"I won't," Nicola promised. And, opening the other half of the door, she came into the shed.

She really liked Edward much the best of her five cousins, perhaps because he was neither brilliant nor beautiful. Certainly not beautiful. Rather short for his age, thick-set, with straw-coloured hair and slightly prominent blue eyes with thick, fair lashes, Edward might have been a beautiful baby or might later develop into a striking-looking man, but as a little boy he was entirely unremarkable.

As Nicola watched him now, absorbed once more in his work, she thought how nice it must be to be so supremely independent of outside considerations. On impulse, she asked him:

"Edward, do you think I'm a very *ordinary* person?"

"Yes," Edward said, without looking up.

"Oh, dear!"

He did look up then, in some surprise.

"What's the matter? Don't you want to be ord'nary?"

"No. Of course not. Do you?"

"Uh-huh. I think extraord'nary people are silly."

"Well—not *extraordinary*, exactly. But it must be nice to be unusual."

"Why?" Edward hammered in a nail with care and accuracy.

"I suppose," Nicola admitted, "because it's nice to be admired and noticed."

7

"I don't think it's specially nice to be noticed," Edward said. "It usually means people want you to do something for them."

Nicola laughed.

"Well, your sisters are all unusual, Edward."

"Yes," he agreed without enthusiasm, and went on with his work.

Nicola leaned her head back against the wooden side of the shed and thoughtfully passed Edward's "unusual" sisters in mental review.

Yes, there were no two ways about it. Her four cousins—Anne, Bridget, Caroline and Diana—were quite, quite unusual. They were known in the district as "The Round Alphabet" since Aunt Katherine—by what she herself considered a charming conceit—had given them names which followed each other in strict alphabetical order.

If anyone could be said to enjoy being left a widow with five children and a host of responsibilities, then Aunt Katherine had enjoyed it. She managed her family, her house and her small but well-kept grounds almost with one hand. The other was free to manage anything or anyone else that came within the orbit of her good-tempered and efficient personality.

Naturally she was the mainstay of the local church, the women's institute, and the young people's guild. And she was the kind of woman who really enjoyed making apple jelly in the morning, decorating the church for Harvest Festival in the afternoon, and lecturing to the Women's Institute on "Social Conditions in the Fiji Islands" in the evening. ("Though really, my dear, I only began to read up my subject properly about midnight last night.")

You couldn't possibly help liking Aunt Katherine. Or rather, you could possibly *dis*like her. She was genuinely kind-hearted, and it was literally true of her that she never sent away anyone in trouble without help. Why should she?—since solving other people's problems was her hobby.

It went without saying that when her niece Nicola had been left an orphan two years ago, Aunt Katherine fell upon the problem as a dog might fall upon a juicy bone; worried it amiably and contentedly, picked it clean of all extraneous matter, shaped it to her own satisfaction, and finally buried it, because (having been solved) it no longer required attention.

Aunt Katherine's late husband and Nicola's father had been brothers. Sometimes Nicola thought that if Uncle Ralph had been of the same dreamy, easy-going temperament as her father, Aunt Katherine must surely have contributed something to his early decease. But she invariably dismissed the thought again as unkind and unworthy.

Nicola could hardly remember her mother, but she had lived a delightful, aimless, haphazard existence with her father, in a little cottage on the Cornish coast. From the time she left school until her father died, three years later, Nicola had been his constant companion. In her last year at school she had even learnt shorthand and typewriting so that she might help him in his work, for in the last years of his life his eyesight failed rapidly.

"My late brother-in-law wrote books," Aunt Katherine sometimes used to explain to people. "No, no, my dear—it's no good asking me the titles. They weren't books that people *read* exactly. Philosophical works,

9

you know. The kind that are reviewed lengthily but unhelpfully in *The Times Literary Supplement*. Quite a genius," she would add absently. And then, still more absently: "So was my dear husband, of course."

Anthony Round might have been an unpractical genius (or might not), but he had certainly contrived to make his daughter happy for the first nineteen years of her life. The only mistake he ever made in his handling of her had been his last move of all, when he consigned her to the care of her only relation, Aunt Katherine. And even that seemed all right in theory, of course.

Aunt Katherine had not seen her young niece since she was a child, but at one word of summons she was naturally only too delighted to swoop from one end of England to the other, for the sole purpose of putting her affairs in order.

Financially, alas, there were very few affairs to put in order, for the philosophical books had indeed brought in very little money. But to Nicola's timid suggestion that there was no reason why she should not earn her own living, Aunt Katherine returned a firm, kindly and absolutely inescapable "No".

"Of course, dear child, there is no reason why you should not do so later. But at the present moment your place is with your only relations. I should not have a moment's peace if I thought I had left you homeless and without any sort of responsible guidance at a time like this."

Nicola said it was very nice of Aunt Katherine. And Aunt Katherine said it was the *only possible course*, and could Nicola contrive to be ready the next day, because she had promised to distribute the prizes at the local school the day following that, and unless the second batch of strawberry jam was cleared off before the end of the week, the berries would be past their best?

And so, without the slightest chance of regretful lingering over the past, Nicola came to live at Longheedon with Aunt Katherine, the four unusual daughters, and the unremarkable but rather lovable Edward.

Nicola cupped her chin on her hand and gazed thoughtfully at Edward now, as he hammered and sawed and chopped with great gusto. He never made much fuss of her, but she had the very definite impression that he liked her, whereas, with his sisters, she always felt that they were much too deeply absorbed in their own important affairs to accord her more than a fleeting, though well-intentioned, moment of attention.

This was particularly so with Anne, perhaps. Anne had taken a double first at Oxford, and though she never, never did anything so crude as boast about the fact, Nicola sometimes used to wish there were such a thing as a single third, and that Anne had taken *that*. She was private secretary now to the local M.P., and Nicola often wondered whether she contrived to make him feel as ill-educated as she made her feel.

Bridget was the sports and social genius of the family. She had already won her bronze medal for skating, and none of the Rounds saw why she should not be a gold medallist one day. She had played tennis at Wimbledon, and was a ballroom dancer of exhibition standard, and Nicola had never seen her make an ungraceful movement in all the two years she had lived in Aunt Katherine's house.

Caroline was "our budding artist", as Aunt Kather-

ine said. But, to tell the truth, she had not only bud-
ded, she had flowered. Her strangely beautiful water-
colours had figured at no fewer than three London
exhibitions, although she was only twenty-two. And
on each occasion her work had been sold.

And then there was Diana. Diana was, quite frankly,
what the Americans call "dumb", but she was so engagingly aware of the fact, and so absolutely beautiful
that it hardly mattered at all.

"I suppose by the time Mother came to me she'd
worked out all the brains of the family," Diana used
to say with a contentment that exasperated her sisters.
"And by the time she came to Edward, the brains *and*
the beauty had been used up."

She had almost sapphire-blue eyes, ash-blonde hair
which owed nothing whatever to "rinses", and a com-
plexion of the kind often described in advertisements
but seldom found in real life. She danced well (though
nothing like so well as Bridget), could listen with an
entirely spurious air of intelligence while a man talked
to her, and could sit and look beautiful with a com-
pleteness that was almost an art in itself. Of the four
sisters, Nicola definitely liked Diana best.

It had been hard indeed to take one's place in a
circle of such charm and talent when one was nothing
but a brown-haired, brown-skinned young nobody,
with long, hazel eyes and a boyish figure that was slim
to the point of skinniness. And even now, after two
years, Nicola still felt oddly like a stranger in a strange
land.

Of course the plan for earning her own living had
never materialized. There was so much to do, helping
Aunt Katherine to manage everything and everyone.

Nicola wrote letters, ran messages, helped in the house, weeded in the garden, picked the fruit for Aunt Katherine's enthusiastic and interminable jam-making and, in fact, did all the unspectacular jobs which everyone else was much too clever to do.

"Really, I don't know what I should do without Nicola," Aunt Katherine used to say with characteristic generosity. But Nicola knew quite well what she would do. She would manage splendidly. Aunt Katherine always did.

"What's the matter?" Edward asked suddenly. "Aren't you happy?"

"Yes, of course," she said hastily.

"Why?"

"What do you mean—'why'?"

"Well, why are you happy? You don't seem to have much reason to be."

"Of *course* I have, Edward." Nicola spoke with guilty vehemence. "I don't know what you mean."

"Well, there's Anne, giving herself the airs of a Cabinet Minister, and Bridget getting her name in the *Sports New*s, and Carrie painting those awful pictures of hers *and* selling them, and Di smirking around like an advertisement for toothpaste. But you don't do anything, and you've just been saying you want to be unusual. It must be fierce watching the others do what you want to do yourself. You'd better get married. That's what people usually do when they aren't much good at anything else."

Nicola couldn't help laughing at these refreshing views on matrimony.

"There isn't anyone to play the part of the bridegroom, though," she pointed out.

"Huh, girls can always get a husband if they try hard enough," declared Edward.

"I expect I'd better go in and do those notices for the Hospital Fete," Nicola said lazily, but she still lingered a few minutes longer.

"Why doesn't Carrie do them?" Edward asked suddenly. "It's an artist's work, isn't it?"

"Oh, not exactly." Nicola felt Caroline would have been affronted at the suggestion. "I can do them quite well enough, I think. Besides, Caroline will be busy enough for the day. She's going to do silhouettes, you know."

"I don't think they'll make much money," Edward said suddenly. "They do too many ord'nary things. Who wants ord'nary lucky dips and stalls with tea-cosies and dolls being raffled? I told Mother a very good idea—something quite out of the ord'nary, but she wouldn't hear of it."

"What was it?" Nicola inquired with some curiosity.

"A competition to see who knew the most swear-words. Fivepence entry fee, and tenpence for anyone who wanted to be audience. I bet you'd have got a lot. But Mother seemed to think the Vicar wouldn't like it. I don't know why, because he must know a good many himself. Lots of the best ones are in the Bible."

Nicola laughed again as she stood up and stretched herself.

"Edward, you'd cheer anyone up," she declared, ruffling his already untidy hair.

"I thought you said you didn't need cheering up," Edward said, but she saw he was gratified.

The two days before the Hospital Fête slipped away

14

in a fever of planning and confusion, reduced miraculously at the last moment to complete order by an almost entirely unruffled Aunt Katherine.

"There now! Look what beautiful sunshine," she exclaimed, as though personally responsible for it, just as the whole family were about to set forth. "The reward of virtue, one might say. After all, it *is* a noble cause." Aunt Katherine overlooked the fact that the same noble cause had been known to be rewarded with a deluge in other years.

Longheedon Hospital had originally been a big manor house, standing in its own grounds, and it would have been difficult to imagine a more delightful place for a fete. Everybody, of course, knew nearly everybody else, and it was all very much in the nature of a huge family party.

Perhaps, Nicola thought a little guiltily, that was why she felt somehow out of it all. Or perhaps it was just her ridiculous shy and reserved disposition which was responsible for that. She felt nervous and overwhelmed, as she always did at this kind of gathering. The fact that her cousins moved so easily among people, gathering praise and compliments as they went, somehow made her feel terribly inadequate and dull.

"It isn't that I want so *much* notice or even a great deal of admiration," thought Nicola. "But I wish someone would look at *me* as though I were something a bit out of the ordinary, instead of as though I were a not very ornamental gate-post."

"Dear Mrs. Round"—("Miss Pottington, of course," thought Nicola, without even turning round from the plants she was carefully unpacking for her aunt's gar-

15

dening stall)—"how nice to see *all* your girls here."

"Yes, my dear. I don't know what we should do without them." (That was the Vicar's wife, perfectly sincere and delighted to be giving praise where praise was due.)

"Oh, not at all. Not at all." Aunt Katherine laughed pleasantly, in a protest which was not intended to be taken seriously by anyone, because *she* didn't know what the fete would have done without them, either. "Of course it *was* very fortunate that Anne was able to persuade Sir Charles to open proceedings. But then she works very hard for him."

"And then Caroline doing those *clever* silhouettes—"

"And, dear Mrs. Round, the idea of exhibition tennis matches. *So* original——"

"—Diana looking enchanting. She looks almost good enough to eat—like the strawberries and cream. Ha, ha!"

"Ha, ha, indeed!!" thought Nicola without mirth. "I wish I were not a nasty, mean, envious——"

"I say," drawled a pleasant, rather lazy voice beside her. "Can you tell me where to spend the requisite amount of money at this show, with the minimum amount of embarrassment and waste of time?"

Aware that she was a good deal flushed with her exertions, Nicola straightened up from bending over a wooden box of plants. In front of her stood an extremely good-looking and extremely amused young man in a light-grey suit. The sun glinted on his thick, fair hair, which was in curious contrast to his darkly tanned skin. His smiling brown eyes took in the scene with obvious appreciation, and then came to rest once more on Nicola with still more obvious appreciation.

16

That alone would have told her—had she not been well aware of it already—that he was a complete stranger in the district.

"Well, you'll find almost anyone willing to relieve you of your money," she assured him with a smile. "But as to the waste of time"—it was her turn to allow an amused glance to travel over *him*—"and, still more, the amount of embarrassment involved, I don't know that I can give you very good advice. What *does* embarrass you, by the way?"

"Meaning that you don't really believe I'm capable of being embarrassed?" he grinned.

"I shouldn't like to have to do it."

"Oh, I'm sorry. I was hoping you would take me for a shy soul who needed piloting round."

Nicola smiled sceptically and went on with what she was doing, because Aunt Katherine would expect everything to be in order when she returned from her consultation with Miss Pottington and the Vicar's wife.

"You just don't believe in me in that role?" suggested the young man determinedly, but with his desire to keep up the conversation so engagingly obvious that Nicola had to laugh.

"Not in the least," she agreed. "Can I sell you some promising rose trees?—or a nice hefty vegetable marrow which you can lug around with you all the afternoon?"

"God forbid!" he exclaimed with a fervour that would have delighted Edward. "Is there a sweet-stall, or something of the sort here?"

"Of course. Under the big elm tree over there. And you'll probably find a couple of nice old ladies near who will be willing to show you round."

He made a face at that, but strolled off at last, leaving Nicola to wonder a little why she had conducted the conversation on quite such friendly and bantering lines. She supposed it was because he was a complete stranger, and therefore entirely unaware that she was the uninteresting member of the Round family. It had been very pleasant to spend those gay few minutes unrestricted by the ever-present awareness of her own inferiority. Almost like the old happy days when there was no opinion but Father's to consider—and he, of course, had always thought one dear and amusing and wonderful.

"Well, Nicola dear! Everything ready?" Aunt Katherine was beside her again. "Splendid! What should I do without you? We've decided to *raffle* that sack of potatoes. That gets over the difficulty of weighing out separate quantities. Of course Mrs. M. will object on principle, but then some people always object to something, and I do really feel that God would rather see people enjoy a harmless little flutter like that than have good food wasted. Because they *would* be wasted."

Nicola agreed that God would almost certainly take this broad-minded view of things, and turned her attention to a small girl who, it seemed, had tenpence to spend, had no intention of spending it at the vegetable and plant stall, but did not mean to part with any of it until she had inspected everything on sale at the fête.

In the next ten minutes there was a fairly regular flow of customers and gossipers, and it was with some surprise that Nicola turned once more to find the fair-haired young man waiting patiently at the back of her

18

stall, evidently determined to speak to her again.

"Hallo. Have you bought your acid drops already?" she inquired absently, as she counted out money into the improvised till.

"No. But I bought this—for you." He held out a box of chocolates which—Nicola knew perfectly well—had been the centrepiece of Mrs. Robinson's sweet-stall.

"But I——" Nicola flushed, and laughed a little nervously. "Thanks awfully. But I don't think I can take it. I mean——"

"You mean, you'd like to embarrass me," he countered promptly.

"Not at all. *I'm* the one who ought to be embarrassed."

"Nonsense. You ought to encourage me to spend my money for the cause."

"But does it have to be spent on chocolates for someone you don't know?"

"I feel no urge towards the purchase of kettle-holders, tea-cosies or babies' vests."

"I see. Not a family man?" Nicola smiled.

To her surprise, a faintly hard expression came into his laughing eyes, and his mouth tightened slightly.

"Not in the least," he assured her curtly. And then: "Please be friendly and accept the chocolates," he begged.

Nicola accepted them, since there seemed nothing else to do, but that was by no means the end of it, for he added at once:

"And you will have tea with me later, when you're not selling rose-bushes and marrows, won't you?"

"Very well," Nicola agreed, half-amused, half exasperated "But do run along now, or else I shall give someone wrong change. Come back about half-past four."

"I will," he promised, with becoming meekness, and took himself off at last, leaving Nicola to deal with her customers in a mood that was somehow very different from the one in which she had started the afternoon. She felt gayer—happier—more confident, she supposed. She even managed to find it nothing more than amusing when Miss Pottington said:

"Dear Nicola, how *proud* you must be of your aunt and your cousins."

At half-past four, to the minute, her would-be escort was back again at her side and, handing over the management of the stall to Aunt Katherine, Nicola went with him to the large marquee where Diana was looking much more conspicuously beautiful than any of the other girls serving tea.

"Don't you think it might be a good idea to know each other's names?" Nicola glanced at her companion with a smile.

"Of course. Mine is Piers."

"People usually have two names," Nicola reminded him gravely.

"Oh, well—if you insist——" he shrugged. "Piers Mason is the whole name."

"And mine is Nicola Round."

"Oh——" He looked at her with even greater interest. "So you're one of the famous Round sisters. That explains it."

"Explains what?"

"Please spare my easy embarrassment," he begged

without a trace of confusion. "Explains my immediate feeling of attraction towards you, of course. I understand you're a wonderful family. All do something remarkable—isn't that it? Do tell me what you do. I'm sure you're the bright and particular star of the family firmament."

It was at this point, of course, that Nicola ought to have explained that she was nothing but the inconspicuous and ungifted cousin, of no particular importance. But she didn't want that expression of fascinated interest to leave Piers Mason's face and, anyway, she felt in a strangely reckless and light-hearted mood. She could not have said afterwards whether it was mischief or bravado or just the sheer desire to hold this amusing young man's attention which made her answer as she did.

Smiling thoughtfully, she said:

"I don't know about being the bright and particular star. I write, as a matter of fact."

"Do you really?" He seemed extraordinarily interested. Just a little too much interested for Nicola's comfort, and she began to regret the absurd position. "I didn't hear that any of the sisters was a writer."

"I'm not 'one of the sisters'." Nicola explained, in a sudden desire for truth on that point at least. "I—I'm a cousin."

"Oh, I see. I pity you," he added with fervour. "Fancy having four cousins!"

"Five," murmured Nicola.

"Five, then. How grim. Cousins are dreadful relations, I consider. That's *my* cousin over there."

Nicola glanced with some curiosity across the marquee, as Piers Mason gave a disparaging nod in that direction.

"The man talking to Sir Charles, you mean?"

"Um-hm."

"Surely he's a good deal older than you?"

"Oh Lord, yes! Quite ancient."

"Well, I shouldn't have put it that way. That one streak of grey is rather distinguished, I think, and you often see very dark people go grey quite young."

"I dare say." Her companion's interest in his cousin was evidently strictly limited.

"You're not a bit alike." Nicola smiled, as she glanced from the fair, lounging figure opposite her to the very dark, grave, authoritative man who was talking to Anne's employer.

"No, thank heaven!"

"I shouldn't want to be a stiff, joyless prig."

"Well, no, I can understand that. Is that really what he is?"

"Um-hm. But don't let's talk about him. We're so much more interesting."

"Are we? I think your cousin looks interesting. I should say he's a personality— in a slightly frightening way."

"Frightening? Ye-es, I suppose one could call him that. Certainly when he's in one of his sarcastic moods it's nicer to be on the other side of the county."

"Oh, he's sarcastic among other things, is he?"

"Disgustingly so at times. *And* intolerant, *and* a bit of a woman-hater."

"I'm surprised you go about with him," Nicola said gravely. She thought a large grain of salt could probably be taken with this hastily expressed opinion, but it was true that the man with the slightly tired, disillusioned eyes might indeed be something of what

22

her companion declared. All the same, he did look a personality, as she had said, and she felt more than a stirring of interest in the two oddly contrasting cousins.

"Go about with him!" her companion repeated scornfully. "No, I shouldn't choose to, in the ordinary way. But for several years he was more or less my guardian and he's never been able to get over it. I quite often stay at his place still and, as he's a friend of Sir Charles, we were both invited over here this week-end. Besides, Sir Charles is rather a decent old boy, you know. He's going to see about a job for me in——Oh, damn!"

"What's the matter?"

"Only that they *would* interrupt just when we're enjoying ourselves. I'm afraid I must go over, if you'll excuse me a moment."

Nicola glanced across and saw a quite unmistakable sign from the cousin that Piers should come to their table. Privately, she thought it extremely rude and high-handed of him to interrupt a *tête-à-tête* tea-party like that, but she gave Piers a slight nod of permission to leave her.

She glanced idly round while she was waiting for him to return, and saw that Sir Charles and his companion were getting up from the table where they had been sitting, and Piers was looking slightly restive and annoyed. A moment later both cousins came across to her.

Reluctantly—even a little sulkily—Piers made the introductions, and the cousin bowed formally and unsmilingly to Nicola.

"I'm terribly sorry, Miss Round"—Piers made no attempt to call her Nicola in front of his cousin, she noticed—"Sir Charles has had an urgent business call and I have to go with him."

"Will you allow me to take over the pleasure of seeing that you have tea?" the cousin said, in that cool tone of his, which expressed no special pleasure—only a grave politeness.

"Oh, it is quite all right, of course," Nicola explained hastily. "I had almost finished, in any case, and I must go back to my stall."

"No, please don't hurry away, or we shall both feel responsible for having spoilt your tea." The cousin sat down opposite her while Piers said a hasty good-bye and added, rather unexpectedly:

"But I shall be seeing you again, of course."

Before Nicola had time to decide just what that meant, he had gone. And almost immediately Diana drifted up with a wonderful smile, to bring fresh tea for the newcomer.

And then, for the first time since Nicola had come to Longheedon, she saw a man look at her beautiful cousin with complete indifference. It was positively intriguing.

"Perhaps," thought Nicola, "he *is* something of a woman-hater."

But if he was, at least he was a polite woman-hater, because he looked after Nicola's wants with perfect attention. Then he said with an air of grave interest:

"My cousin tells me that you are a writer."

Oh dear! This was retribution indeed. Nicola felt her colour rise slightly, but she contrived to murmur something non-committal.

"You look very young for a writer, if I may say so." He smiled at her, but something in the smile reminded

Nicola of Piers saying how sarcastic his cousin could be

Somehow that fired her to defiance, and she decided to play out the ridiculous comedy completely. After all, she would probably never see the man again.

"Yes," she said coolly. "I was only eighteen when I published my first book. I was lucky enough to make —something of a success at once."

"I see. How very interesting." She wished those speculative dark eyes would not look at her quite so directly. "Do you write under your own name?"

"No. Oh, no," Nicola assured him hastily, wondering in sudden panic whether she would have to invent the name of her early masterpiece on the spur of the moment.

"Under what name do you write?"

Her mind went completely blank. She couldn't even think of names like "Mary Smith" or "Janet Brown" at that moment.

"Oh, I don't think——"

"Surely you aren't shy about your own achievements? Do tell me. Believe me, I am genuinely interested."

Into the utter void that her mind appeared to be at that moment floated a name. Not only *a* name, but a name which she had seen on the back of a book. Actually a plausible author's name. She had noticed it idly yesterday when she was changing Aunt Katherine's library book. She could not imagine why it came back to her now, but it did. Completely calm once more, she smiled full at the man facing her.

"No, I'm *not* shy about it. Rather ridiculously proud of it sometimes. My pen name is A. M. Leigh."

"A. M. Leigh," he repeated thoughtfully. "I must remember that. Oh, won't you really have any more tea? Are you sure you don't want anything more?"

Nicola had never been surer of anything in her life. She felt anything else would choke her, and managed to say with absolute firmness that she must go back to her stall.

He rose at once, paid Diana, still without appearing to notice her smile, and escorted Nicola back across the lawn. All the time she was thinking:

"Thank heaven he doesn't belong to the neighbourhood! Whatever induced me to get into such a scrape? Anyway, I'm safe now."

He bade her a grave and still polite good-bye, and left her with an almost passionate feeling of happiness that she was safe back with Aunt Katherine, the rose trees and the vegetable marrows.

As he strolled away again, Anne came over to her mother's stall.

"Hallo. How are you getting on? Did you have tea with Mr. Mason, Nicola?" The faintest note of respect seemed to linger in Anne's usually confident tones.

"Yes."

"How interesting. He's—charming, isn't he?" She glanced thoughtfully across the lawn after the tall figure.

"No," Nicola said curtly. "I like the cousin much better."

"Oh, do you?" Anne was faintly patronizing again.

"Yes. I think this one is sarcastic and unfriendly and imagines he's rather marvellous." She was a little surprised at her own vehemence, but Anne was tolerantly amused—perhaps because she thought she could have managed him much better.

"Oh, well, I suppose he has some reason to think himself marvellous."

"I don't see why he should."

"But, my dear, he *is* rather celebrated, after all. Don't you know who he is?"

"No," Nicola said, very briefly indeed, because Anne's air of superior knowledge was very trying.

"Why, he's A. M. Leigh, the writer, you know. His last book won the Murgatroyd Award for the best novel of the year."

CHAPTER II

NICOLA stared at her cousin in speechless horror.

"I don't believe it," she said at last. But of course she did. It was exactly what *would* happen.

"Don't believe it? Why not?" Immediately Anne was slightly offended that anyone should call in question any statement she had made.

"Oh, I—didn't mean that exactly." Nicola somehow recovered herself enough to hide her chagrin and dismay. "Only he—he doesn't seem like a famous writer," she finished lamely.

"I think anyone would take him for a gifted and cultured man," Anne replied (meaning anyone with any intelligence, of course). "And I certainly don't see why he shouldn't be a writer."

Nicola, knowing Anne's passion for pursuing an argument to its logical conclusion, agreed with desperate haste that her remark had been foolish and ill-judged, and that Mr. Mason might very well be a writer after all—and a celebrated one, at that.

Satisfied, Anne took herself off, and—as most of the visitors were now either at tea or extracting what enjoyment they could from the competitions which excited Edward's scorn—Nicola was free to snatch a few moments alone with her own thoughts.

And very disagreeable and humiliating thoughts they were too!

Why had she been so silly—to say the least of it—as to say what she had to that man? She wondered now what had made her obey that ridiculous impulse.

"I suppose I was just fed up and miserable with always being nobody among people who are all somebody," Nicola thought. "Besides, with *Piers* Mason one could always have turned the whole thing into a harmless leg-pull, if necessary."

With the cousin, she felt instinctively, one could do nothing of the sort. Besides, she had elaborated the whole wretched business so thoroughly when he had driven her into a corner with his questioning. It had become something like a piece of serious deception by the end.

It was too bad of him to have asked her her penname!—And too silly of her to have given him his own!

"Out of thousands—*millions* of names, I had to choose his!" thought Nicola crossly. "I suppose what really happened was that when I was at the library I saw several copies of his wretched book which won whatever it did win, and that was how the name stuck in my mind. Oh, *why* couldn't I have been wellinformed like Anne and known it was too celebrated a book to tack myself on to safely?"

"I could *cry*!" thought Nicola. And two tears actually did squeeze their way into the corners of her eyes as she bent over a box of promising dahlia plants, pretending to herself that she was really only counting the number still unsold.

"Such a charming afternoon! Things could hardly have gone better," commented Aunt Katherine at this most inappropriate moment. And Nicola, blinking back her tears hastily, agreed with what enthusiasm she could that "things could hardly have gone better".

"A most happy speech from Sir Charles," mused

Aunt Katherine, still in a state of general congratulation. "No wonder he is popular. Just the right words for the occasion."

"Yes," Nicola agreed mechanically.

"Most interesting that he should have brought Leigh Mason with him. Anne tells me he is actually A. M. Leigh, the novelist."

"Yes." Nicola wished she could have thought of something else to say.

"I haven't seen him yet myself, but Anne says he is most distinguished-looking." And Aunt Katherine turned away to try to interest a latecomer in the dwindling stock on her stall.

It was at this moment that Nicola saw him again.

He was strolling among the trees, some distance away, presumably having had enough of the fête and sampling instead the pleasures of the very beautiful grounds.

Her first sensation was nothing more than one of sheer discomfort at seeing the cause of her embarrassment once more. Then suddenly she felt an overwhelming desire to extricate herself—at whatever cost to her pride—from the absurd and unhappy situation she had provoked.

Nicola fled.

She was frightened when she realized that she had committed herself to further—and probably even more embarrassing—conversation with the sarcastic Leigh Mason. But anything was better than to go home leaving things as they were.

She caught up with him just as he reached the small stream that bordered the south side of the hospital grounds.

"Mr. Mason——"

Her tone was more timid than she had meant it to be, but he turned at once.

"I—I want to apologize to you." She was a little breathless, but more with nervousness than running.

"Apologize?" Those dark eyes regarded her gravely. "But why?"

"Oh, you—you must know why." She wished he would help her a little, but of course if she had really offended him, he was probably thoroughly enjoying her discomfiture. "I shouldn't have tried to—to pull your leg." (She decided at the last minute to put it that way.)

"But did you?" He allowed an expression of rather unkind puzzlement to appear on his face.

"You know I did. About—about pretending to be a writer and then giving you your—your own name as mine."

"But, my dear," he returned coolly, "that was not a leg-pull. You were perfectly serious about it, and no one, I'm sure, was more surprised than you to find out who I was."

Then suddenly his expression altered. Nicola saw a faint smile cross his grave, dark face, and she had an idea that those cynical eyes softened a little.

"Tell me," he said—peremptorily, but with a touch of real interest—"why did you really do it?"

"It—it was a joke," Nicola insisted unhappily.

He shook his head.

"No. Try again."

"Well, at least, I—I never intended it to develop quite so far."

"I realize that."

31

She didn't know quite how much like an embarrassed child she looked, standing there twisting the belt of her dress in her thin, brown fingers.

Then she felt him calmly take her hands, holding them lightly for a moment in his own strong, fine fingers.

"Don't do that. You'll spoil your dress, you know. And that would be a pity, because it suits you. Now tell me why you wanted Piers to think you were a writer. Was it just to show off a little?"

"N—not exactly. But I don't think you'd understand," Nicola insisted desperately.

"I could try to exercise what intelligence I have," he assured her gravely, and she thought from his tone that he was genuinely amused by now.

"Well—you see—all my cousins are either very clever or very beautiful. *Really* so, I mean. They do deserve to have everyone admire and praise them. It—it isn't that I'm envious—at least, I hope it isn't. But sometimes it's—it's rather discouraging to be terribly ordinary when they—Oh, it sounds so *petty*, put into words!" poor Nicola exclaimed wretchedly.

"On the contrary, it sounds extremely human. Please go on—What did you say your name was, by the way?"

"Nicola Round."

"Oh, yes. I remember. Well, go on, Nicola."

"There isn't very much more to tell," she said shyly. "Piers—your cousin, I mean—said he supposed I was one of the 'famous Round sisters'—everyone knows them in the neighbourhood and no doubt Sir Charles had mentioned them. I—I *think* I meant it partly as a joke—" She met those keen, amused eyes for a moment, and added: "Well, perhaps it was mostly serious. But, anyway, when he asked me what I did, I had a mad impulse to—to pretend *I* was clever, and not just completely uninteresting."

He looked at her in that speculative way, and she waited rather nervously for some dry and critical rejoinder. What he did say, however, was:

"Who gave you the idea you were uninteresting?"

"Well, I'm not specially clever and I'm not specially pretty and——"

To her astonishment, he took her abruptly by her chin and tilted her face up.

"No, you're not pretty," he agreed critically. "You have a very unusual little face, though. Hasn't anyone ever told you that you have real hazel eyes, and that they are almost unknown nowadays?"

It was all done so impersonally that Nicola gasped slightly.

"N-no, no one's ever told me that," she admitted.

He smiled dryly.

"Well, someone has told you now," he said. Then he laughed softly as her thick lashes swept downwards in sudden embarrassment. "I don't think I should worry about the clever and beautiful cousins, if I were you, Nicola," he added rather disagreeably. "I imagine you will find quite enough men to make fools of themselves about you."

There was a short silence. Then Nicola said, without looking at him:

"Am I—forgiven for doing what I did?"

"Is that important?" He sounded amused again.

"I—I think I'd like to know everything was all right again," Nicola said in a slightly troubled way.

"Everything is perfectly all right," he assured her, with that touch of mockery again. "You may go back happily now, my child, and sell your vegetables once more."

She smiled a little.

"Thank you. Good-bye."

"Good-bye. And don't forget about the hazel eyes. But, Nicola—" just as she was turning away. She turned back again—"Don't try using them on Piers." And he walked off along the stream without giving Nicola a chance to tell him just how impertinent she thought he was.

Use them on Piers indeed! She'd use them on anyone she liked, and without asking *his* permission too!

"But he did mean to be kind, on the whole," Nicola decided generously, as she hurried back to Aunt Katherine. "But I see why his cousin isn't exactly affectionate."

Still, it was a relief to know that one had put things right. Because he *had* understood in the end. Understood rather amazingly well, considering he was not supposed to be a sympathetic person.

After that she tried to dismiss the Mason cousins from her mind, in favour of the much more important matter of attending to her part in the Hospital Fête.

At the end of a day which had tired everyone except Aunt Katherine, the family returned at last to the comfortable relaxation of home, pleasantly conscious that they had more than done their duty both by the Longheedon Hospital and the social life of the village.

"Incidentally, one somehow always enjoys these things when it comes to the point," commented Bridget, who had been personally complimented on her tennis by Sir Charles.

"It's the consciousness of duty well done," Aunt Katherine declared, sincerely but mistakenly.

"Oh no, Mother dear," Anne smiled at her with the tolerance which she extended even towards her parent. "With you perhaps, because you have the disposition that makes a hobby of duty. But what Diana, for instance, enjoyed was being able to move about in front of a lot of people, aware that she looked beautiful."

Aunt Katherine, shocked that anyone should attribute Diana's tea-serving to anything but the highest motives, was immediately prepared to counter that. But Diana placidly took the wind out of the maternal sails by the shameless admission—

"Yes, I loved it. And the only person who didn't notice me was the good-looking creature who took Nicola to tea. Or rather, the *second* good-looking creature who took Nicola to tea. How did you do it, Nick?—rope in both, I mean. They were about the only strangers in the place, and certainly the only presentable ones. Fancy managing both!"

"Whatever did you talk about, Nicola?" asked Bridget. "You never have much to say for yourself."

"We talked about books part of the time," Nicola retorted, not without humour, "and writers in general."

"With Leigh Mason, I suppose?" That was Anne.

"Yes."

"Did he tell you he had taken the lease of Thorpe Compton?"

"No," Nicola admitted.

"Why?—Did he tell you that?" inquired Diana.

"No," Anne replied a little stiffly. "Sir Charles told me. I believe he has a certain amount of propaganda work to do for the Government, apart from his literary work, and I suppose Thorpe Compton appealed to him as quiet and a good place for undisturbed and concentrated work."

"And the other one?" Diana wanted to know. "The one who looks more like a human being?"

"Oh, *he's* a bit of a rotter, I believe," Anne said, with less than her usual discretion.

"I dare say that's why he looks more human," was Diana's comment, while Nicola felt an indignant desire to defend the charming Piers from Anne's smug and final judgment.

She was just drawing breath to do so when Edward gave a tug at her sleeve.

"Nicola, come outside, will you?"

Slightly mystified, Nicola accompanied Edward into the hall.

"Here, this is for you." And he produced from the pocket of his blazer a crumpled and rather astonishingly dirty note.

"Thank you." Nicola laughed slightly as she took the battered, folded paper. "But who gave it to you?"

"One of the fellows Di was talking about, I should think. I've never seen him before." Edward was plainly not interested.

Nicola was, however.

"Which one? Was he dark or fair?"

"My goodness, you don't suppose I go about looking at chaps' hair, do you?" Edward said disgustedly.

"All right." Nicola didn't pursue the subject, but took the note upstairs to her own room because, somehow, in what Edward called "a house full of women" it was curiously difficult to keep one's private affairs private.

The note was short enough, she found, when she did unfold it, and signed with the sprawling initials "P.M."

I hated having to go just as we were getting to know each other," the few lines ran, *"but, believe me, the matter really was out of my hands. But we're coming to live in Longheedon at least, Leigh is and I'll darned well see I spend a good deal of time visiting him and then you and I can really know each other. You said you were a writer, but I hope to heaven you're not a very good one. I'm sick of people who do things superlatively well, and you're much too nice to be a budding celebrity. Till no later than to-morrow, I hope—*

P.M.

With a slight laugh of sheer pleasure, Nicola folded up the note again, and stood staring absently out of the window, across the fields to the distant sea.

How odd that someone else should feel as she did— that to be with someone ordinary would be the most delicious relaxation and pleasure. "Sick of people who did things superlatively well!" Yes, that was the feeling exactly.

And he hoped to see her to-morrow. So much so that he had even bothered to write a note about it.

When Nicola went to bed that night, it was with a pleasant feeling of anticipation for the morrow. If life would never again be quite the cloudless, delightfully haphazard affair it had been under her father's management, at least it held some very attractive possibilities still.

The next day everyone was just a little cross—with that crossness which inevitably accompanies the "flat" feeling left after the successful conclusion of an arduous venture. Only Aunt Katherine seemed ready to plunge into fresh activities with her enthusiasm undiminished.

"Nicola dear, I want you to cycle over to the Hall with Anne," she began, almost before she had removed the top from her breakfast egg. "I promised Mr. Curton he should have Sir Charles's own notes of his speech, and it must be in time for the Tuesday *Mercury*—No, Anne, it *won't* do if you bring the notes at lunch time. You know the *Mercury* office closes this afternoon, and that means the notes wouldn't be the e before Monday and the whole account of the fête would be spoilt."

Nicola accepted the commission with a better grace than Anne accepted her company. Jealous of her position as the perfect secretary, Anne resented the presence of any other member of the family on her employer's premises.

However, Nicola was used to her cousin's little ways, and she only smiled as she cycled off with the notes. But just as she rounded the bend which took her out of sight of the house, someone stepped from among the trees at the side of the road and signalled to her eagerly to stop.

The someone was Piers Mason.

"Oh——" Nicola's bicycle wobbled somewhat perilously as she slowed down and dismounted.

"I'm sorry. Did I startle you?"

"No, of course not. I didn't expect you to appear just at that moment, that's all."

"I'm staying here, you know."

"Yes, I remember. You told me."

He stood there, smiling down at her, and suddenly she was happy and most unaccountably excited. Impossible to believe it could be so good just to see someone! Someone who had been a stranger until yesterday too.

"May I walk down the drive with you?"

"Very well." She spoke rather hastily, and they walked on together, silent for the first few moments.

Then he said quite simply:

"It's wonderful seeing you again. But when I am going to see you again?—long enough to have a real talk?"

"I don't know." Her foot was already on the pedal of her bicycle, and she smiled at him.

"Look here, can I come over to your place? Will you be in if I come this afternoon?"

"I expect so."

"Then I shall come. And you *will* be pleased, won't you, Nicola?"

"I'm always pleased to help Aunt Katherine entertain her callers," Nicola assured him over her shoulder as she mounted her bicycle and rode away.

Afterwards she wondered why she teased him. It was most unlike her to do so, and yet there was an element of lighthearted fun about it which suddenly made the day very beautiful and bright and amusing.

"I suppose it's the lovely and novel sensation of having a friend—*my* friend," Nicola told herself. "Not just a friend of one of the girls."

It was quite late that afternoon before she was able

to escape from Aunt Katherine's many commissions, and slip away to her own room for a few minutes. She wanted to change to that green dress of hers which brought out the greeny lights in her eyes. It hadn't been Piers, of course, who had remarked on the colour of her eyes, but—well, perhaps he *had* noticed their unusual colour, all the same.

She glanced at herself in the glass with a good deal more interest than usual.

What was it Leigh Mason had said? "Certainly not pretty—but an unusual little face." Perhaps that did describe the rather fine oval face, with the long, greenish hazel eyes, the singularly red mouth, and the even golden tan of her otherwise colourless cheeks. Her hair was too straight and an ordinary brown, of course, but at least it was fine and smooth. Perhaps if she did it another way—? Or was it best to leave it for the moment, and experiment later when the result was not so important?

Hastily deciding against the new hairdressing, she twisted her smooth brown hair into its usual low knot on her neck, and went downstairs to see how Piers had fared.

Aunt Katherine met her in the hall, but it was obvious at once, from the absence of her smile, that her thoughts were only half on Nicola and half on some other urgent matter which claimed her attention.

"Go along into the drawing-room, dear. Mr. Mason wants to see you. I think he must have mistaken you for Anne, because he said it was something to do with business."

"Mistaken me for Anne indeed!" thought Nicola, but she smiled and murmured something non-committal to her aunt, as she turned away to the drawing-room.

As she pushed open the door she felt a thrill of excitement which she made no attempt to hide from herself.

For a moment she thought the tall figure by the window *must* be Piers because she had been so completely prepared to see him there. Then he turned, and she gave a slight gasp of sheer astonishment.

It was Leigh Mason, not Piers, who had "come to see her on business".

CHAPTER III

THE surprise was so complete that Nicola was quite unable to recover herself immediately.

"Why, I——" She stopped, flushing a little, as he came forward to take her hand. "I didn't—realize you were here," she added in confused explanation, as she saw him regarding her rather quizzically.

"Didn't anyone tell you I wanted to see you?"

"Oh, yes. But I thought——" She stopped again, and this time the flush was a good deal deeper. To her chagrin he immediately guessed the cause of her confusion.

"Oh, I see." He smiled dryly. "You were expecting my cousin?"

"Well——"

"Not on business, surely? I can't imagine Piers voluntarily concerning himself with business."

The touch of sarcasm in that secretly netted Nicola, but she was a little afraid to rush into angry defence of Piers. For one thing, she very much doubted if she were a match for Leigh Mason in argument and, for another, she wondered uneasily just why he had come to see her.

Surely he could not be taking it upon himself to be angry that she and Piers had already pursued their friendship further. It was not in any degree his business. Though that, she felt sure, would not be sufficient in itself to deter him!

He seemed, however, to think he had kept her waiting

long enough for explanations, because, as she hesitated in perplexed silence, he said:

"Shall we sit down?"

"Oh, yes, of course. I'm sorry——" She recollected her duties as hostess. "I'm afraid I'm still woolgathering a little."

"I understand," he assured her gravely. And she had a horrid feeling that he did.

They sat down, and Nicola said:

"Did you really want to see me on business?"

"Certainly." Again there was that slight, dry smile. "I'm not in the habit of making business an excuse for something else. Tell me——" He suddenly became abrupt and to the point. "You were Anthony Round's daughter, weren't you?"

"Yes." Nicola was a little surprised at this reference to her father.

"And you helped him in his work?"

"Well, I typed for him and arranged his manuscripts and that sort of thing. Why?"

"Because I'm going to ask you if you would care to come over to Thorpe Compton after I settle there, and work for me. Not every day, probably, because I shall have to do my own work more or less at odd times now. I have a certain amount of Government work, and that must come first."

"And you're willing to assume that I'm efficient?"

"I can't imagine that Anthony Round was a man to suffer a fool gladly—even if she happened to be his own daughter."

"Well, no," Nicola agreed with a smile. "Daddy was pretty exacting where work was concerned. I think I'm a good deal out of practice, though."

"You could remedy that quite quickly, I take it."

He seemed rather determined to have her, Nicola thought, and there was something extremely heartwarming about that. The idea of having a job of her own—a degree of importance!

"Well?" Leigh Mason was watching her with attention and—as so often—a touch of amusement. "It requires a good deal of careful thought, eh?"

"Oh—no! I was just thinking what a heavenly idea it was."

His eyebrows went up at that.

"My dear Miss Round"—no mention of "Nicola" this time—"you are singularly easily pleased. And we haven't even discussed terms yet."

"No, I know. They hardly seem to matter because——"

"How very unbusinesslike of you," he said with a smile.

"Well, I mean, I should agree to almost anything so long as I could get back to a definite job—something I know how to do and which I can take hold of as my own."

"I see. And you don't mind the idea of working for me? I suppose I ought to warn you that I am sometimes difficult to work for. But perhaps Piers has already implied that."

The last was a statement rather than a question, and Nicola chose to consider that it needed no reply.

"I think," she said with a smile, "that I should be prepared to work for the Devil himself, if it were really a regular job of my own."

"I trust," he retorted gravely, "that I shall never give you reason to wonder if that is indeed what you

44

are doing."

"Are you *so* difficult?" She could not entirely suppress the unusual dimple which appeared at the left corner of her mouth whenever she was specially amused.

"I think," he told her, "we will leave that for you to decide for yourself later. It would hardly be politic for me to destroy your nerve beforehand. And now about salary."

To Nicola, with nothing but her small dress allowance, what he offered seemed munificent. He assured her amusedly, however, that the terms were not extravagant.

"I am sure that Sir Charles, for instance, pays your cousin a considerably higher salary," he said.

"Oh, but I'm nothing like so efficient as Anne," Nicola explained anxiously.

"You relieve my mind," he assured her dryly. "Would you be prepared to start in about a week or ten days' time?"

"Yes, of course. That would give me time to finish up anything Aunt Katherine specially wanted done, and also to get up some sort of speed at my work again."

"Then I'll let you know when I want you." He was already very much the employer.

"Yes. And I think I can come almost at a moment's notice. Mr. Mason—it's awfully kind of you."

"I told you—kindness has nothing to do with it." He smiled slightly as he gave her his hand. "And I can assure you that you will find me much less than kind if you are not reasonably efficient."

"I'll do my best," Nicola promised.

And, at that moment, Piers walked in.

"Hallo, Nicola—oh, hallo, Leigh. Sorry, but it would be ungraceful to withdraw at a moment's notice. And what—if I may be unpardonably inquisitive—is my charming cousin doing here?"

Nicola was a good deal embarrassed by this contretempts, but Leigh Mason not at all.

"As you see—concluding a very pleasant call," he said, a little coldly. "Good-bye, Miss Round. Please don't bother to see me to the door." And with the slightest nod to his cousin, he took his departure.

"Hm-hm. I suppose that's what the dramatists call 'making a hasty exit'," Piers remarked. "I trust I haven't interrupted a scene which should have been left *un*interrupted."

"Don't be ridiculous," said Nicola, as though she had known Piers Mason all her life. "We were discussing business."

"Seriously?"

"Seriously. Shall we go into the garden? We can talk better there."

By common consent they strolled down the centre path to the small orchard at the end of the garden.

"This is where I come when I have some time to myself," Nicola explained, as she seated herself in the low crutch of a very old apple tree.

"Then it was specially sweet of you to bring me here," Piers said, as he threw himself on the ground at her feet and smiled up at her. "But do tell me—what did Leigh really want? To make trouble?"

"Oh, no. He genuinely came on business. No one was more surprised than I was, I can tell you. He wants me to be his secretary. At least, I suppose that's what one would call it."

"He—*what*? Damned impudence!" Piers sat up indignantly.

"It's not! I think it was rather good of him to give me the chance."

"You don't mean to say you're going to accept?"

"Of course. Why not?"

"Because it would be a sin for anyone as pretty and gay as you to work for a slavedriver like Leigh. And anyway——"

"Yes, I know. You're going to trot out the bit about my being a writer. I'm not. That was a leg-pull. I'm sorry, Piers, but please don't be upset and annoyed about it. I'm feeling on top of the world."

That time Piers laughed much more in his old gay, amused manner.

"All right, Nicola, you win. But if he tells you I'm a graceless scamp——"

"I shall reserve judgement until I've settled that for myself," Nicola finished for him, and they both laughed. "I thought," she added, with a touch of smiling reproach, "that you would have been pleased, rather than so unflatteringly dismayed by the arrangement."

"Why on earth should I be pleased?" he wanted to know.

"Well, I—most mistakenly, no doubt—thought you might like to see me about the place and——"

"Nicola! I really am a cad! Of course that will be wonderful. I don't know why I sulked and made objections. I wasn't thinking of that side of it. I——"

"It's all right," Nicola laughed. "You needn't go into any more detail. You're quite forgiven, and it's settled that I accept the post with your full approval.

47

Now come in and be introduced to Aunt Katherine. And don't make any disparaging remarks about my future employer in front of her, because professional loyalty will force me to defend him."

"Very well." Piers got up with a smile, and taking both her hands, drew her to her feet. Just for a moment she was very near to him—a little too near perhaps. Then he had released her hands, and they went into the house together.

In the end, it was almost a fortnight before Nicola received her summons to Thorpe Compton, and during that fortnight the most strange and delightful change took place in her life.

To begin with, Aunt Katherine—who never did things by halves—completely ceased to make any demands on her time. Nicola's guilty appeals to be allowed to help in her usual tasks were met with the cheerful assurance that:

"I must get used to doing without you, dear child. And in any case, you need all the time you have for getting up your typing speed and that sort of thing. I don't want Mr. Mason to find you anything but satisfactory."

Having decided to dispense with Nicola's help in future, Aunt Katherine positively enjoyed coping with the inconvenience of any new arrangement. So Nicola, cheerfully thwarted at every turn, finally accepted her good fortune—and found that she had more than enough time to pursue her delightful friendship with Piers.

They took long walks together, along the river valley to the sea, on the one side, or over the great heather moors which stretched away to the west, on the other. Most of the time they talked—sometimes arguing passionately about some topic on which they disagreed—but occasionally they would be silent, with that deep, pleasant silence which goes with absolute companionship. Once he took her hand in his and swung it lightly as they walked along, and all the time—and even afterwards when he had let go her hand again—Nicola was overwhelmingly conscious of the feel of the strong, warm fingers on hers. Even then he seemed to hold so much more than her hand in his.

He told her a good deal about himself—how he had been an only son, and lost both parents before he was in his teens.

"That's where old Leigh comes in," he explained. "There wasn't anyone else to guide and direct my young life, so he took it on himself to act the parent and guardian."

"He must have been quite young then," Nicola said.

"Oh—yes, I supose so. I can't remember ever thinking of Leigh as young. He's a good twelve or fourteen years older than I am, you know. He must be thirty-six or seven now."

"Even so, he must have been rather young to take on the responsibility of bringing up a schoolboy."

"I don't think Leigh ever minded responsibility," was what Piers said to that, and Nicola thought that was undoubtedly the truth.

On the Sunday before she was due to start her first week's work, she went walking over the moors with Piers. He told her that the household at Thorpe Compton had more or less settled in by now. "And the only thing needed now is to have you about the place," he added.

"I shall be busy working most of the time," she warned him.

"Yes, I know," he said, but without much conviction, Nicola thought. She saw that it would be she who would have to make sure that discipline was preserved.

It was when they were on their way home that he said:

"Come round by Thorpe Compton with me, Nicola. I'd like to show you what a difference it has made, having the garden cleared. It had got ito a terrible state."

"Yes, I know. But"—she hung back slightly—"I think I won't come this afternoon."

"Why not?" He looked surprised.

"Well, your cousin might feel I was making rather free of the place, considering that I'm going to be an employee there from to-morrow onwards."

"Oh, nonsense." Piers laughed easily. "*I'm* asking you there this afternoon."

"No, please—I'd rather not."

"Well, at least come down as far as the hawthorn hedge at the end of the garden. That can't be out of bounds, even to your sense of fitness."

Nicola came, still with slight misgiving, though she felt it would be ridiculous to make more of the point, and she found herself wishing that Piers would not hold her arm in quite such a friendly manner. After all, they *might* meet her employer anywhere round here, and he *might* be annoyed by the whole position.

"There! How's that for a ten days' clearance?" Piers indicated the garden very much as though it were his own.

"I can't see. At least, not much," Nicola said, as she reached up on tiptoe to see over the tall hedge.

"All right, here's a six-footer at your service," Piers declared and, putting his hands round her waist, lifted her as though she were a little girl.

"Piers! *Please* put me down!"

"Why? You can see nicely now, can't you?"

"Yes, but it's so—so frightfully undignified."

The next moment she was in his arms and he had kissed her.

"Now talk about dignity," he said, and he was not smiling any more, but rather frighteningly serious.

More startled than thrilled by the way he kissed her, Nicola leant back against his arm, looking at him with wide eyes.

"Piers, why——"

"No, don't ask me why I did it," he interrupted curtly. "I couldn't help it, that's why. And, any-way——"

"I'm sorry to interrupt," Leigh Mason's voice suddenly said rather coldly. "But won't you bring Miss Round into the garden? It seems a little inhospitable to keep her standing out here."

Nicola, really frightened now, swung round to find her employer standing quite close behind her and, if an air of cool reserve could be said to convey extreme anger, she thought Leigh Mason was very angry at that moment.

"Oh, good lord!" exclaimed Piers. "Can't you mind your own business?"

"Miss Round *is* my business," was the cool retort. "Or she will be from to-morrow."

That annoyed Nicola and, on the spur of the moment, she said sharply:

"Thank you. But I can look after myself very well."

"Possibly so." The ironical smile which he gave her was not reassuring. "I admit that if you want to—enjoy yourself with anyone else, it's hardly my business. But if you choose my cousin for the purpose, then I claim a certain amount of responsibility for what happens, and——"

"You needn't say any more." Nicola knew she must be white with anger because her cheeks felt strangely cold, but he seemed unaffected by that.

"I should like to say one thing more. Has Piers told you the particular reason why it's extremely unwise to be quite so—friendly?"

There was absolute silence and, glancing at Piers, Nicola saw that he, too, was white and angry and, in some tragic way, baffled.

"Well?" Leigh Mason addressed his cousin now, not Nicola. "Will you tell her, or shall I? For I insist on her being told."

Still there was silence, and then, with a slight shrug, he turned back to Nicola.

"As a married man, Piers has no right to be kissing my secretary—even if it does happen to be one day before you enter my employment."

CHAPTER IV

IT was useless to try to think of anything which would really gloss over the situation. Nicola glanced in agitated silence from one to the other of the two men. Then she did what seemed to her the only possible thing to do. Turning to Leigh Mason, she said coldly:

"Thank you for the information, since I'm sure you gave it with the best intentions. But perhaps it would be as well to leave Piers to explain his private affairs himself."

Leigh shrugged.

"As you like. But forgive me for saying that I think a considerable amount of explanation is called for." Then, in quite a different tone—the tone of an employer—he added: "I shall expect you to-morrow at half-past nine." And, turning on his heels, he opened the high green gate and went through into the garden of Thorpe Compton.

Only then did Nicola turn her full attention on Piers.

She had hardly known which was the more acute—embarrassment on her own behalf at the assumption that she had any special interest in Piers, or embarrassment on his behalf that he should be caught out in this humiliating manner. Now that she looked at him, however, she was shocked by the hard unhappiness and anger in his face, and she felt a wave of pity—illogical though it might be—which threatened to swamp any other feeling.

He made no attempt to avoid her glance, and his

53

frank, unhappy eyes made her want suddenly to re-assure him.

"I'm sorry," he said baldly before she could speak.

"For what, Piers?" She spoke quite gently.

"Oh—everything. The foul scene Leigh made, for one thing. And not having been frank with you from the beginning, and—kissing you when I had no right to, I suppose."

With an effort, Nicola produced a careless little smile.

"Oh, come, don't let's make so much of a thought-less kiss. I see your cousin attached a lot of importance to it, but I don't think either of us did." She saw he wanted to interrupt her there—possibly to insist that it had not been unimportant—but she gave him no chance to speak, and hurried on: "As for your being married, I don't know that there was any reason why you should let me in on your private affairs. I sup-pose—" she looked at him doubtfully—"Is it not a very successful marriage?"

"Hopeless," Piers told her curtly.

She saw from his expression how relieved he was that she was taking it all so calmly, and she felt thank-ful she had managed to conceal her real sense of shock and dismay.

By common consent, they fell into step together, walking slowly away from Thorpe Compton in the direction of Aunt Katherine's house.

"Would you care to—tell me about it?" Nicola was diffident about saying that, but she thought he was badly in need of sympathy.

"Yes. If you won't be bored."

"Of course not. I'm awfully sorry things have gone

so badly for you. And I'm afraid your cousin isn't exactly sympathetic."

"Oh, Leigh!" Piers gave a short laugh. "Leigh doesn't know the meaning of the word sympathy."

Nicola thought that was not entirely correct, when she remembered one or two things he had said during that unfortunate episode at the fête. But she let that pass.

"Do you—see her at all, Piers? Your wife, I mean."

"No, I haven't seen her for over a year. It was one of those idiotic one-week affairs that I suppose are rather apt to happen to my particular sort of fool. I don't want to sound as though it was all her fault. We were utterly and absolutely unsuited, but it was I who forced the pace, so I've only myself to blame."

"Did she—leave you?"

"Yes. For someone who could give her a much better time. She was a good-time girl in every sense of the word, and it takes a pretty solid bank balance to keep up with that. We lived up to the edge of everything we had for the few months we were together. I'm an engineer, you know—" he added in parenthesis— "and a good engineer can clean up a very satisfactory packet most times, particularly if he has a few out-of-the-way ideas of his own. She was all right so long as everything went well. Then she met someone with more money than I shall ever have—and that was that."

Nicola hesitated for a moment, and then said:

"Are you going to divorce her, or—or——"

"I suppose so," Piers shrugged. "You can, after all, say the marriage has irretrievably broken down. But it takes time. And meanwhile," he added rather savagely, "Leigh considers himself the keeper of my conscience."

"Oh, Piers, I am sorry. You've had a perfectly rotten deal." Her slight touch on his arm held a great deal of unspoken sympathy. "At least don't bother any more about what happened this afternoon. It's not at all important—and I do understand."

He put his hand over hers for a moment and pressed her fingers hard.

"You're a darling, Nic. But it was important, you know. I meant that kiss more than I've ever meant anything."

She was silent for a moment, in something between pleasure and dismay. They must not go any further, of course, as things were—but she was glad he had meant it.

"Well?" He was smiling slightly now, more like his old self—rather as though he knew her dilemma and wanted to tease her a little.

"I don't know quite what to say to that."

"You're not angry?"

"N-no, of course not. Only I don't think it's much good our talking like that, is it?"

"Why not?" He looked obstinate.

"Well—" she smiled suddenly, with a touch of real mischief—"I don't want to sound like your cousin, but —you *are* a married man."

"And as such, must keep myself severely *to* myself, even if the aforesaid wife has decamped with another fellow?"

"Piers, I'm so sorry. But, after all, we haven't known each other so long that the freshness has worn off a mere friendship, have we?" She smiled very winningly at him. "Don't you think we could be satisfied with that for the time?"

He laughed—a little vexedly, she saw.

"You certainly plead well for a wait-and-see policy," he told her. Then, as though his usual good humour entirely re-asserted itself: "You're a darned good little friend, Nic. And don't think I don't value your friendship. I promise not to do a thing that would embarrass you—or shock poor old Leigh. How's that?"

"It sounds almost too circumspect to be interesting," Nicola declared. And at that they both laughed, and the tension of the scene relaxed completely.

Only when they reached the gate of Aunt Katherine's house did Nicola feel again the sense of restraint which this episode had inevitably put upon her. Before, it would have been the most natural thing in the world to ask him to come in, and probably stay to tea. But—without even putting it into words—she knew that the family were already inclined to view Piers as what Diana called "an attachment". Whether they thought that way or not would hardly have mattered before. But now it would never do to have that idea going about. Longheedon had a special and terrible interest in anyone who "got herself talked about with a married man, my dear".

The next morning Nicola set off for Thorpe Compton with very mixed feelings. It was wonderful, of course, to be beginning a real job at last, but she couldn't help wishing that she were going to work for someone who was more or less a stranger, rather than someone with whom she had already had some very disconcerting encounters.

"The business at the fête wouldn't have mattered so much," Nicola reflected. "But I do wish yesterday—Oh, well, never mind. It can't be helped. I should think he's the kind to be frightfully impersonal over work, so there's no need for me to start getting self-conscious."

This turned out to be nothing less than the truth. So far as she could judge from early impressions, Leigh Mason seemed likely to prove a good employer. Certainly he expected plenty of work from her and a high standard of performance, but he was clear in his explanations of what he wanted done and extremely patient about seeing that she understood exactly.

Never once during that first morning was he anything but the impersonal employer, and certainly nothing in his manner suggested that their last encounter had been highly personal—not to say embarrassing.

Nicola felt very well satisfied with life, and was already nearing the end of her work when Piers—announced by the very slightest tap on the door—came into the room.

"May I come in?" he inquired, characteristically having come in first.

"Well, I'm busy, but—Why are you laughing?"

"Oh, just the complete picture of the conscientious secretary."

"But I *am* a conscientious secretary, Piers. At least, I hope so. And it's perfectly true that I'm busy."

"You mean to say Leigh plunged you headlong into it the very first day?"

"Well, why not?"

"Oh—no reason, I suppose—except that no one else would expect you to take things anything but easily the first day."

Nicola smiled, but only slightly.

"Piers, don't talk as though I'm only fit to play with this job," she said rather earnestly. "You don't know how good it is to be working at something definite and —and progressive again. Not just dozens of little odd jobs that hardly need doing in any case."

"Yes, I do." He smiled in return, but as though he really took her seriously this time. "I feel just that way about my own work. But you must let me tease you a little too."

Nicola laughed then—but she immediately wished that Piers would go away, rather than sit on the side of her desk with an air of intending to stay for some time. She didn't want to be priggish or self-important about her work, but—suppose her employer did come back at this moment. He would be bound to think that she just wasted her time with Piers as soon as he himself was out of the way.

"All right, I don't mind your teasing me," she assured him. "But not in my employer's time, please."

"Good lord! I believe you said that almost seriously!"

"I did."

"Nic, your degree of conscientiousness is almost terrifying."

"Oh, it's not only that. It's——"

"*I* know what it is," Piers declared, with an air of having stumbled upon a great truth. "You're scared to death of old Leigh."

"I am *not* 'scared to death of old Leigh'," Nicola retorted sharply. "Only——"

She stopped suddenly in complete dismay, for the door, already ajar, had opened to admit her employer.

59

It was quite impossible to tell from his expression whether or not he had heard this last remark, but to Nicola's horrified eyes he looked grimmer than ever. However, he ignored her, addressing himself to Piers, who got off the corner of Nicola's desk with a very faintly disconcerted air.

"Are you—using Miss Round's services as a secretary?" he inquired crisply.

"Oh no, I only——"

"Well, I am. You don't mind, do you?" and he held the door open pointedly.

Piers laughed annoyedly and shrugged.

"Well, don't start pitching into *her* about it," he said. "It was entirely my fault, I'm afraid. She's been spending the last ten minutes trying to get rid of me."

"Indeed? I'm sorry you took so much getting rid of. But perhaps you'll go now."

"Oh, all right!" Piers's tone was on the very edge of insolent, and he made a sympathetic little grimace at Nicola before he finally took himself off.

Nicola trembled very much for the moment when she should be left alone with her employer once more. She was very much afraid that some dry reprimand would be forthcoming. But Leigh Mason merely picked up some of the work she had been doing and, taking it to the window, proceeded to examine it at his leisure. After a while he said:

"This is good. You've been very well trained, Miss Round."

Nicola felt herself flush with gratification, and something suspiciously like relief.

"I—I'm glad you're pleased." She spoke a trifle more subduedly than she had intended.

60

"You must have worked very hard this afternoon."

Nicola glanced at him quickly to make sure that this was not meant sarcastically. But Leigh Mason's grave dark eyes regarded her with a suspicion of kindliness.

"I like the work very much, you know," Nicola told him earnestly. "And yes, I did work hard."

She supposed she had very much wanted to please him, because after all he *had* given her this precious chance. And she had so unfortunately been put in the position of appearing to waste her time. She was indescribably relieved and touched that he seemed willing to give her the benefit of the doubt and not to read any dreadful meaning into the scene he had interrupted.

But it seemed she had experienced complete relief just a little too soon, for a moment later Leigh Mason went on:

"At the risk of seeming an elderly spoilsport, however—" Nicola winced slightly at the tone of that, sure now that he had overheard the end of her conversation with Piers—"there is one thing I must stress. I do not intend to have my cousin making free of this room."

Nicola made as though to speak, but he stopped her with a slight movement of his hand.

"No, I know it was not your fault this afternoon. I'll speak to Piers himself about that. But, apart from anything I can do, you will have to take a firm stand from the beginning, you know."

"Please—" exclaimed Nicola, loath to let Piers shoulder all the blame—"please don't think I want to suggest it was only his fault this afternoon. I, too——"

"No." Her employer smiled dryly. "I'm quite sure you don't want to suggest anything of the sort. But after having known Piers for a good many years, I really don't need any 'suggestions' on that point."

"Mr. Mason," Nicola said with desperate boldness, "I think you're very hard on Piers."

"Oh?" His tone was polite, but his eyebrows rose rather frighteningly. "In what way?"

"Almost every way." Having once committed herself, Nicola thought she had better do the thing thoroughly. "You seem determined to think the worst of him always. I—I've never heard you anything but sarcastic and critical about him."

To her surprise, Leigh Mason actually looked startled rather than annoyed.

"Do I—really strike you like that?" he said slowly. And then, more sternly—"or is that just what Piers says?"

"No, it isn't just what Piers says. I do use my own judgement too, occasionally, you know, and I can't help thinking——" she stopped suddenly. "I'm awfully sorry. This isn't my business at all, of course."

"No, of course not," he agreed absently. "But go on."

"Well, I can't help thinking that Piers could hardly be anything *but* defiant and provoking when you so obviously show that you think him rather a hopeless person. It doesn't exactly encourage anyone to be anything else, you know."

"You don't think a man should ever reach a point where he completely loses patience, eh?" He smiled slightly.

"You mean yourself, I suppose, by 'a man'?"

"Yes."

"But has Piers given you *so* much cause to lose

patience? I know you were more or less his guardian, and I can imagine he wouldn't be the easiest of wards. But then——"

"—I shouldn't be the easiest of guardians?" suggested her employer.

"Well"—Nicola's deprecating smile was disarming, "*you* said it."

He laughed rather shortly.

"You plead extremely well for someone you don't know much," he said, not very kindly.

"But then I'm really very sorry for Piers," Nicola told him. "He—he told me all about—what you said yesterday, and it's not a very happy story, Mr. Mason."

"No. But then a man must expect to pay for his own folly," was the curt reply.

Nicola looked at him speculatively and said:

"I always think the reflection that one only has oneself to blame is about the most uncomforting one there is."

"Maybe. But that doesn't give one the right to shirk payment."

"Mr. Mason, Piers is not the only man to have made an unhappy marriage, and certainly not the only one to have made an unfortunate mistake. I suppose nearly all of us do things we wish very heartily undone at some times in our lives. Even you must have."

"*Even* I?" His smile made Nicola go scarlet.

"I'm sorry. I——"

"Please don't apologize. I'm sure I have only myself to blame for this," he said, with a touch of humour which Nicola would hardly have expected in him. "But, as you suggest, it would be foolish to insist that 'even I' have not made mistakes at some time or another. They have not, however, included a perfectly ridiculous marriage, at breakneck speed and against all the advice of my friends and relations."

"It was—as bad as that with Piers?"

Leigh Mason suddenly seemed to become aware of the fact that his cousin's private affairs had received an unjust amount of attention.

"Well, it was very much like that. But I don't want to deepen your impression that I have nothing but ill to say of Piers. He was a headstrong young fool but, as you say, not the only one. Perhaps I have been hard and unreasonable sometimes, but I see, Miss Round, that with an observant young person like you in the house, I shall have to mend my ways."

Nicola glanced at him rather anxiously to see how much sarcasm was wrapped up in that but, on the whole, she thought he meant it more than half seriously.

"I suppose," she said reasonably, "it's never easy for people of entirely different temperaments to judge each other tolerantly. After all, the kind of mistake Piers made is certainly not the kind you would fall into."

"Thank you for the compliment to my common sense, but why not, exactly?"

"Well, you're—I mean, Piers, said—"

"Yes?" He had been examining her work once more, but he glanced up again now with casual interest. "What did Piers say I was?"

"S-something of a woman-hater."

"Indeed? Well, I haven't much opinion of some of your sex," he informed her with brutal coolness, "but I hope I'm nothing quite so silly as a woman-hater. Now I think it's time you went along home, Miss

Round. You've had a sufficiently taxing first day."

Nicola thought so too! And bidding her employer a rather hasty good-bye, she set off home across the fields.

She had hardly got farther than the end of the hedge which surrounded Thorpe Compton, however, before Piers hailed her, with a cheerfulness undiminished by the afternoon's reprimand.

As she waited for him to come up with her, Nicola wondered again at the extraordinary attractiveness of his fair hair and tanned skin. No wonder Piers had made the particular kind of mess he had of his life! Probably most women ran after him. And, thought Nicola honestly, small blame to them.

"Well—" He smiled down at her, "did Leigh play the dragon?"

"No," Nicola confessed. "No, I can't exactly say he did. In fact, now I come to think of it, I believe *I* did most of the lecturing."

"You—what? Oh, Nic, you're delicious! What did you lecture him about?"

"The way he treats you."

"You darling! What on earth did he say?"

"He said he'd have to mend his ways," Nicola explained, a sudden dimple appearing in the middle of her cheek.

"I don't believe it!"

"Well, it wasn't quite as simple as that, of course. But I believe he experienced a slight twinge of conscience about his behaviour towards you. Though he told me—and this is quite serious, Piers—that you mustn't come in while I'm working. That's perfectly reasonable, you know, and I hope you won't make any trouble about it, because I'd hate to quarrel with you."

"You wouldn't do such a thing about Leigh, would you?"

"Let's say—about my work. And I would if—if you really made trouble."

"Is the work *so* important?"

"Yes. You know it is to me." She glanced at his rather discontented face. "Piers, you mustn't mind. Why shouldn't it be important?"

"Because you were made for something ten thousand times more romantic and wonderful than just banging a typewriter for my wretched cousin—and one of these days I'll tell you what it is."

CHAPTER V

DURING the next few weeks Nicola gradually took the measure of her new life—and found it very good. She was happy in her work, happy in her new-found sense of independence, but happiest of all in her friendship with Piers.

It was useless to remind herself that he was married and that, however remote and shadowy his wife might be, she did, in fact, exist. Nothing about him suggested the essential limitations attaching to a married man, and it was impossible to regard him as such. Except when he deliberately reminded himself of his position (and those times were few) he was gay, inconsequential, unfettered—and entirely devoted to herself.

The friendship could hardly go entirely unnoticed at home, of course. But the fact that she worked for Leigh Mason at least supplied one reason for her being on good terms with his cousin.

Edward perhaps regarded the situation more seriously than anyone else. But Edward, after all, was a particularly serious-minded person. He tackled the question one Sunday afternoon, when Nicola had looked into his favourite wood-shed to tell him that tea was ready.

"Yes, I'm coming," he assured her absently, without any sign of moving.

"Well, hurry up, there's a good boy. I specially want tea over early because I'm going out.'

"With Piers?"

"Well—yes, as a matter of fact. Why?"

Edward got up slowly and brought his full attention to bear on her.

"Are you thinking of marrying him?" he inquired, with characteristic lack of finesse. "Because I was just thinking that if you are——"

"Edward! What on earth are you talking about?" Flushed and startled, his cousin turned on him quickly. "You mustn't say things like that. You—you give people horrid, uncharitable ideas, and then they begin to gossip and—and, anyway, it's ridiculous!"

"All right." Edward was unmoved. "I was only going to say that *if* you thought of marrying him, you'd better know—he's married already."

"Who told you that?" Nicola spoke sharply.

"Nobody did. Miss Pottington told Mother, and I happened to hear her."

"Wretched old gossip!" muttered Nicola savagely.

"Miss Pottington? But she always knows," Edward pointed out, not without a certain admiration for Miss Pottington's efficiency in this respect. "You'd think she looked into a crystal and saw things, like those people who tell fortunes," Then he added: "So you knew about him being married all the time? Well then, I needn't have bothered."

Nicola smiled irresistibly.

"Nice of you to have 'bothered', Edward, but—no, really"—she suddenly became unnecessarily earnest about it—"you needn't 'bother' as you put it, in the very least. Why, Piers and I are very good friends, but absolutely nothing else at all."

"Well, of course"—Edward gazed at her in a slightly owlish manner which was faintly disturbing—"you couldn't be anything else, could you? That's why I thought you ought to know. Because if you marry anyone who's got a wife already that's bigamy. At least, it's bigamy for him. And you go to prison for bigamy—several years sometimes."

"Quite," agreed Nicola crisply. And after that she hustled her little cousin in to tea, reflecting as she did so what a singular talent Edward had for repeating an unfortunate word with impressive frequency.

However, it would have taken more than Edward's tactlessness to upset her at the moment. She was looking forward immensely to her evening with Piers.

After tea she changed quickly into her cream trouser suit—one of the very good things left from the days when Daddy indulged one rather absurdly. Fortunately, things like that hardly "dated" at all—and perfect tailoring was always perfect tailoring.

She twisted a bright green scarf round her hair, glanced in the glass and knew—why not enjoy the fact? —that she looked her very best.

It was twenty minutes' brisk walk to the place where she was to meet Piers, but on an evening like this every step was enjoyment.

She was less than half-way along the road when Piers' rakish little two-seater appeared over the brow of the hill, shot down the slope at breakneck speed, and came to rest beside her.

"Hallo." She smiled as he leant forward to open the door for her. "You got away early, then?"

"You bet I did. I didn't mean to waste any of this perfect evening if I could help it. And you've been lazing in the garden all day, I suppose?" He ran an appreciative eye over her cream suit.

"Wrong, Mr. Mason. I've been working remarkably hard for your cousin, who wanted umpteen thousand words typed before Monday and specially asked me to go across to Thorpe Compton and get them done to-day."

"I thought you were only supposed to have a five-day week," Piers said as he started the car once more.

"But I don't mind a six—or even a seven-day week if it's necessary."

"No wonder old Leigh says you're a good secretary. You're always giving doses of soothing syrup to his self-esteem."

"Does he say I'm a good secretary?" Nicola spoke eagerly.

"Yes, something like that."

"Oh, Piers, do tell me. What did he say?"

He grinned. "Oh, well, it was when he was lecturing me about not wasting your time, and he got very grandfatherly and pompous——"

"I'm sure he didn't!"

"All right. Fatherly and smug, if you prefer that. And he said: 'I don't want her spoilt. She's a good child, and she's a remarkably good worker too.'"

"Oh, Piers, that was rather nice of him." Nicola clasped her hands in her lap, and smiled straight ahead, as though she saw something very pleasant on the long white road in front of her.

Piers glanced at her curiously.

"You get on very well with Leigh, don't you?"

Nicola laughed slightly.

"No, I don't know that I could say that. Oh, we don't *quarrel*, of course. We're not on that footing, for one thing. I suppose—I suppose it's really that I value

70

his opinion." Nicola was faintly surprised herself to discover that. "And I'm glad he thinks well of me—quite apart from wanting to give satisfaction in my job."

Piers didn't say anything for a moment. Then, when he spoke, his tone was abrupt.

"Do you value my opinion?"

"Why, Piers"—she turned to him with a smile—"of course I want you to like me, and—and——"

"But it's not the same thing?" he suggested.

"Well——"

"Why is Leigh's opinion more important than mine?"

"Oh, Piers, it *isn't*!" She was distressed. "You're just twisting things round. I only said what I did—about valuing his opinion, I mean—because, I suppose, one feels instinctively that his standards are unusually high, and it's gratifying to hear that one comes up to them."

Piers's easy sense of humour re-asserted itself.

"No qualms about *my* standards being unusually high, I notice," he remarked with a grin.

Nicola gave a relieved little laugh.

"Perhaps that's why you're so much more comfortable to be with." Nicola slid down a little farther in her seat and made herself comfortable. "You don't really suppose I would prefer to share this heavenly evening with Leigh, do you?"

"No, of course not." He looked entirely satisfied again.

"Where are we going?" Nicola inquired lazily, after a few minutes.

"To the lake at the foot of Errodene Quarry."

"Oh, Piers, that's too far!"

"No, just far enough."

"But we shan't be home until after dark."

"Yes, we shall. You haven't been driving with me before, Miss Round, or you wouldn't worry about that."

"Sure?"

"Quite sure."

By the time they reached the lake, the sun was sending bright shafts of light down the evening sky— the final blaze of glory before it sank behind the bank of clouds that were gathering now in the west. They stood there—their arms rather tightly linked together— watching the golden reflection shorten across the waters of the lake.

"I'm glad we were in time for this," he said softly, and Nicola just nodded, with a deep sigh of satisfaction.

The rim of the sun slowly disappeared behind cloud, the last flicker of golden light vanished from the lake. And suddenly there was the first hint of twilight, and the world had grown perceptibly colder.

"Piers, we must go! It's getting late—and I don't like the look of those clouds."

"There's no hurry," he said lazily. "It won't be really dark for ages yet."

"No, I know. But it's going to rain."

"Nonsense. It couldn't rain on 'our' evening."

"Yes, it could. Please, Piers!"

For some reason she could not possibly have identified she was strangely frightened, and that gave urgency to her words.

"All right." Laughing a little, he allowed himself

to be persuaded. But even so, he would not let her hurry back to the car—detaining her instead by slipping his arm round her waist, and strolling slowly along the bank of the lake.

"You shouldn't run away so quickly from the good things, Nic," he told her teasingly. "The bad ones are always waiting round the corner, anyway."

"You don't really think that, do you?" Nicola was shocked.

"What? That we have downs in this life as well as ups?"

"N-no. *That*, of course. It's only natural. But you spoke as though—oh, as though the shadows were always waiting, and we only walk in the sun and enjoy ourselves when we are foolish enough to forget realities."

"Well, isn't it something like that?" Piers was oddly serious for him.

"No, Piers, of course not. That's a dreadful idea. Why, no one would ever plan for a happy future if they thought that. How could they?"

"Some people don't plan for the future, Nic. I know I don't," he said carelessly. "I take what is good today, and don't reckon to whine if tomorrow is bad."

"But——" She was silent suddenly, quite unable to put into words what she was thinking, because one thing which he had said had cut clean across all theoretical arguments.

Some people don't plan for the future, Nic. I know I don't.

It was ridiculous to feel so chilled and dismayed. Of course, Piers was like that about *almost* everything. Gay and careless, with a day-to-day philosophy. That

73

was part of his charm. She had known about that all along. Only it was rather different when it came to a question of settling *their* future. Where that was concerned, unquestionably he looked ahead and planned.

At least—did he?

"How quiet you are, Nic." He tightened his arm affectionately.

"Yes, I know. I was just—enjoying the last of the scene."

"Sorry now that you decided to hurry away?"

"No. I think we must go. We have a long way to go."

"And a good, speedy little car in which to do it," he reminded her with a laugh. "There she is, standing at the top of the path. Not much to look at, but she's never let me down yet. I'm darned fond of that car, you know, Nic. I bought her with the first big commission I made, and I'm almost sentimental about her."

Nicola laughed, and some of the sense of strain went. This was how she liked Piers best. Smiling, talking nonsense, and being the gay companion she understood. He was very silly and sweet about his car—especially considering it *was* rather battered. But, as he said, it certainly went well. Nicola ran an appreciative eye over it as they came near—and then suddenly she gasped and clutched Piers's arm.

"What?" He looked surprised.

"Piers, look! It's been leaking. There's a big pool, and I think——"

"Hell!"

Piers leapt up the last few yards of the path, and by the time she came up with him he was already muttering and getting out tools.

"Is it serious?"

74

"If you call being stranded miles from anywhere with half a pint of petrol serious—it is."

"Piers, what on earth——?"

"No, don't ask me, darling. Because I don't know the answer to that one. I'm just trying to stop the leak before the whole lot's gone."

Nicola stood by silent—partly because she was afraid of distracting him from the urgent task, partly from sheer dismay. If they really had next to no petrol left——

She glanced over the deserted landscape. It had seemed so bright and friendly and warm when they had come here less than an hour ago. Now it seemed chill and barren, and the clouds, which had been picturesque while the sun was setting, looked sullen and menacing now.

She turned back to the car again with nervous eagerness as Piers straightened up.

"Have you managed to stop it?"

"Yes. But there's not enough petrol to get us half a mile."

"Then what——"

"I don't know."

"Do you mean we can't get home to-night, Piers?"

He gave her a worried glance and then, leaning over the door of the car, he pulled out a map which he began to examine anxiously.

"No. We couldn't get as far as Polhaven, which is the only place where we could even hope to pick up a train."

Nicola, too, hung anxiously over the map, which he had spread out on the bonnet of the car. And then, as they searched for familiar names within reasonable distance, first one large drop of rain, then another and another fell with a vicious "plop" on the map.

"Oh, damn!" Piers folded up the map hastily. "Here, get in, Nic, while I put up the hood. What filthy luck! It's going to be a soaker."

Nicola, however, helped him to put up the hood before she squeezed into the seat beside him once more.

"Well, that settles that!" Piers pressed his lips together. "We can't spend the night out now, even if we chose to."

"Spend the night out! Why, Piers, of course we can't. Surely we have enough petrol to get us to some sort of inn or pub or something."

He cocked a quizzical glanced at her.

"You a citizen of Longheedon and not more alive to gossip than that!"

"Oh, but—Piers, how ridiculous! We can't be the first people to be stranded like this. And anyway, who is to know us, if we *do* turn up together at any place near here? We might be——"

" 'Mr. and Mrs. Smith of London', in the time-honoured formula," Piers finished dryly.

Nicola laughed.

"No, certainly not. But I don't expect we shall have to give our names, come to that."

"In these days one usually has to sign some sort of hotel register. And I must say I don't relish doing that."

"Piers, I think you're exaggerating things. I know it's all very horrid and stupid, but we haven't done anything wrong, and the same thing *must* have happened to other people. Besides, this isn't 1875. It's——"

76

"I know, my dear. But I happen to be a man who is desperately anxious to divorce his wife. You don't suppose I'm exactly eager to go about signing hotel registers in company with another woman, do you?"

"Oh, Piers, I'm sorry! I didn't think. But—but how could anyone know?"

"I don't *know*, Nic. It's only that fate can be so damned ironical. Oh, I'm being a fool, I expect—and confoundedly inconsiderate to you. Forgive me, darling——" He caught her hand quickly. "I'm just exaggerating, as you say. And I know it's a rotten position for you as well as me. There's nothing to do but make the best of it. We'll go back along the road until we find a likely place, and then we must just go in and tell the best tale we can."

"I think so. And don't worry, Piers. Nothing could happen. I'll just telephone Aunt Katherine as soon as we get there, and tell her we'll come back by train as early as we can to-morrow."

"Right."

Piers's tone sounded cheerful again now, but she noticed there were a couple of worried little lines between his brows as he let in the clutch.

For the first couple of miles they drove in silence. Then he spoke rather abruptly:

"Nic."

"Yes?" She glanced inquiringly at him.

"I'm going to use a different name, and I want you to do the same. It may be fanciful and cowardly and all that, but I'm damned if I'm going to take any risks over this business, either of spoiling your reputation or —or delaying my divorce."

"But, Piers, it seems so—well, as though we'd got something to hide."

"No one need ever know. It's the names in the register that stick in my throat. Once we've cleared out tomorrow morning no one can tack this adventure on to us, but if our names are left side by side in a book that anyone can look at—Nic, you must see how silly it is!"

"Very well."

Nicola hated agreeing to what seemed to her a cheap and unnecessary subterfuge. But there *was* Piers's position to be considered, and she could see that this adventure might cause him a good deal of anxiety.

"And I'm hanged if *I* want to be mixed up in a divorce suit, come to that," thought Nicola.

"Very well, Piers." she repeated. "I'm Mary Martin, for the purposes of this one night," and she gave a little giggle which she could not altogether suppress.

He smiled faintly, but not as though the situation caused him any real amusement. And they drove on in silence, until a swinging sign at some cross-roads informed them that they were outside The Coach and Four.

"Just as well," murmured Piers, "for I think *our* coach is about to founder altogether. That is, if a coach can founder."

They left the car outside on a piece of open ground near the side of the road, and went into the small entrance-hall of the inn.

Evidently it was not a place that did much regular business, and presumably relied for its trade on casual travellers like themselves, who required either a meal or a bed for the night.

The middle-aged man behind the reception desk

eyed them with singular lack of interest, and Nicola thought:

"Well, there's no awkward curiosity here!"

He even took their explanation about being stranded without displaying any of the avid interest which Piers's anxiety had led her to expect.

"Supper and two single rooms? Yes, we can do that all right."

"And I want to telephone," Nicola broke in eagerly. "That's very urgent. I'd like to do it right away, please. Where is the phone?"

"It's out of order, ma'am. I'm sorry."

"Oh well, it can't be helped. We'll stay." Piers turned back to the man, who languidly dived under the desk and produced a battered exercise book.

"You might sign the register." He pushed it towards Piers, who took out his fountain pen.

For one moment Nicola felt genuine amusement, for she knew Piers was trying to think of some sufficiently common name.

Then the man added as an afterthought:

"Oh, and I'll see your banker's card, too. I'm assuming you'll be paying by cheque, sir?"

CHAPTER VI

FOR a moment Nicola thought Piers was going to refuse to produce his banker's card. Then even he must have realized how ridiculous the risk of that would be, compared with the hundredth chance of anything unfortunate following on the admission of their real names.

As she went up the stairs, Nicola turned to glance over her shoulder at Piers. He was standing at the desk, holding his banker's card in his hand and saying something which had actually made the man behind the desk laugh. Evidently he had completely recovered his spirits and, in that case, thought Nicola with relief, he was probably no longer bothering about their being stranded like this. She realized now that she had instinctively shrunk from being identified in Piers's mind with anything which had caused him worry or embarrassment.

The room which she was shown was at least clean and, if there was nothing particularly attractive about it, it also was inoffensive.

She washed her hands and face at the fixed basin by the window. As she stood there, drying her hands, and looking out of the window at the rain-drenched garden, a knock sounded on her door.

"Come in."

"May I, for a moment?" It was Piers's voice, and his tone was urgent.

"Yes, of course," She turned round to face the door as he came into the room. "Is anything wrong?"

"No, nothing's wrong. I only wanted to speak to you alone for a moment before we go down to the dining-room. There's an inquisitive chambermaid snooping around, and we shall probably find in a place like this that she waits at table too."

Nicola laughed.

"Oh, never mind. What did you want to say to me?"

"Only don't use my name when you speak to me. At least, not if you can remember."

"Oh, Piers, why ever not?" Nicola suddenly felt exasperated. It was all rather ridiculously like some bedroom farce on the stage, she thought. "Your name's written now as large as life in that register, whether you like it or not. Why worry about it any more?"

"My name isn't written in that register." Piers spoke with unwonted curtness.

"Not written? But don't be silly. I saw you ready with your fountain-pen just as I finished signing—and your banker's card was in your hand."

"Yes, Nic. And it stayed there. I kept my thumb over the Christian name, though our friend down there didn't notice that—and I signed the book in my virtuous cousin's name."

"Oh, Piers, you shouldn't have done it."

"But why not? Why not make old Leigh useful to me for once in his life? No one will ever be any the wiser. You were laughing at me ten minutes ago yourself because you thought I took the whole question of risk too seriously."

"Yes, I know. But that's different. To use your cousin's name deliberately like that—masquerade as him when you're doing something rather risky, anyway —it isn't right."

81

"Oh, come——" Piers shrugged, his easy good humour entirely restored by the trick he had played. "Who masqueraded as 'A.M. Leigh' herself, come to that? Rather funny to think we've both taken his name in vain."

"All right. I suppose there's nothing more to be said about it. But I'm not going to pretend I approve."

In spite of everything, however ,they contrived to have a singularly pleasant evening.

The small private dining-room into which they were shown turned out to be unexpectedly comfortable, and the meal, though unpretentious, was well cooked.

The rain which beat upon the windows had turned the summer evening into something .cold and dreary, but a fire was lighted for them, and the thick curtains which blacked out the windows also shut out every vestige of the cold, unfriendly night. Sitting side by side on a comfortable, shabby settee, drawn up to the fire, Nicola and Piers shared perhaps the pleasantest and most intimate hour which had yet fallen to them.

She told him something of her life before her father died, and he, in his turn, talked for the first time about his work. She saw then what was—or at any rate, had been until now—the real love of his life. He might talk disparagingly about work in general or pretend that he thought she was too conscientious about her own work —but it was perfectly obvious that his heart was in his job. He spoke of machines as though they were living things and, as she listened, Nicola felt herself beginning to think so too!

At half-past ten it became obvious that the people of the inn believed in moderately early hours, and they said good night to each other and went to their rooms.

With the slightest encouragement, she knew, Piers would have kissed her good night. But that encouragement was not forthcoming. Life had become just a little too puzzling already for Nicola's liking, and she was not going to complicate it further by any kisses.

In spite of the strange room, the anxiety about her people at home, and the dilemma in which she had landed herself, Nicola slept well, and woke to a brilliant, sunny morning from which all sign of the previous night's storm had disappeared.

She got up quickly and dressed, breakfasting in her room as she and Piers had decided the evening before. After all, there was no need to court attention among whatever people patronized the inn for the sake of the breakfasts for which it was "famous".

At a quarter to nine she decided to go downstairs and see what was happening. They would have to set off as soon as possible in search of a garage. On the way downstairs she met the chambermaid.

The girl stared so much that, for the sheer necessity of saying something, Nicola spoke abruptly.

"Will you please knock on Mr. Mason's door and tell him I've gone down—and that it's a quarter to nine already."

"Yes, miss." The girl hurried on upstairs and Nicola went down into the sunny hall.

"Dear Nicola! _How_ extraordinary! Who would have thought of meeting you here—and at this time in the morning too!" exclaimed a delighted voice. And, Nicola found herself face to face with a beaming Miss Pottington.

"Why, hel-lo, Miss Pottington. I—I'm just as surprised to see you." Nicola somehow got that out, and contrived to smile with something like naturalness, but all the time she was thinking: "What on earth am I to say to her? Suppose Piers comes down the stairs at this moment! I must think of something! Quick—quick!—But what?"

"Such a *small* place the world is," she declared brightly. "Here have I been visiting my dear brother —almost the other side of the country, as one might say, and we were driving back to Longheedon. We made a *very* early start and we stopped here for breakfast, and who should be the first person I see—miles from home—but *you*, dear Nicola? And now what are *you* doing so far from home at this hour in the morning?"

It had come! The dreadful moment of explanation.

But while the avalanche of Miss Pottington's own explanations had been falling round her, Nicola had been using her wits. She would have to lie—and lie pretty heartily. Almost without a tremor she smilingly answered Miss Pottington.

"I've been staying overnight with an old school friend, quite near here. We, too, came out very early and thought we'd call in here for breakfast. I believe they're famous for their breakfasts at this place," she added in smooth parenthesis.

"Yes. Yes, indeed they are," Miss Pottington confirmed. "Now isn't that delightful? We can *all* have breakfast together, and——"

"Oh, but I'm afraid we've just finished. Too bad!"

"Really? Oh, dear, dear, isn't that a pity? But never mind. In any case, you must meet my brother. Where *has* he got to?" Miss Pottington glanced round over her shoulder.

And in the one moment's pause, the still somewhat vacant-looking girl approached Nicola and said with a dreadful, stolid distinctness:

"Mr. Mason's still in the bedroom, miss, but he said to tell you he'd be down in five minutes."

Miss Pottington pivoted slowly round to face Nicola again, as though propelled by some irresistible mechanism.

For a moment they said nothing—simply faced each other in speechless horror which, if different in cause, was equal in effect.

In a sort of guilty helplessness Nicola stammered into inadequate explanation.

"The—the car broke down. We——"

"I think," Miss Pottington said majestically, "that I will *not* ask my brother and his wife to meet you, Nicola." And, turning away once more, she made her way towards her brother as though she were retreating from some pressing danger.

For a second Nicola was tempted to follow her and insist that she heard a fuller explanation. But it was impossible to create something like a scene in a public place like this. Besides, what would Miss Pottington, of all people, think of the real facts? It was because she knew so fatally well how they would be received that Nicola had not given them at first. Now it was too late. Doubly, trebly too late!

With a feeling of despair, Nicola made for the stairs. At least she must see Piers and tell him what had happened. They might be able to think of something. Piers was resourceful. There must be *some* way——

She met him on the upstairs landing, coming along humming and smiling as though he hadn't a second thought now for the awkward situation in which they were placed. Evidently he already considered the danger past—though certainly, at the expression on her face, his smile faded.

"What's the matter, Nic?"

"Listen—something dreadful's happened. Miss Pottington, of all people in the world, has turned up and——"

"Blast! Where is she?"

"Still in the hall, I think." Nicola leaned over the bannisters until part of the hall was within her range of vision. It included the reception desk and, standing there, examining the register with an air of shocked attention, stood Miss Pottington.

Nicola gave something like a groan.

"What is it now?" Piers leaned over the bannisters in his turn.

"Don't you see? She's made some excuse to look at the register. Piers, I could *faint*!"

"Well, that wouldn't help. Thank God I used Leigh's name, at least. That means——"

"Piers, don't be so disgusting! How dare you be so callous about involving your cousin in a scandal—let alone me too."

"But, my dear, steady on! There's no need to run away with the most sensational explanation. Surely you can put it over that you were travelling as Leigh's secretary—the car broke down (God knows that's true enough!)—and——"

"No! It's no good. She'd pumped me already and I got panicky and tried to pass the whole thing off as a week-end with a school friend. Then that idiot girl came up and twittered something about Mr. Mason still being in the bedroom (not even '*his* bedroom', Piers, but '*the* bedroom') and that he would be down in a minute."

"Good lord!" Even then Piers's sense of humour was a little too much for him, and he grinned faintly. "What on earth did the old girl do?"

"Looked at me as though she suddenly smelt a dead rat, and as good as told me her fifty-year-old brother wasn't old enough to know my sort."

"Did you try to explain?"

"Oh, I *tried*, Piers. But it was much too late, of course."

"Of course." Piers looked thoughtful. "Nic dear, I'm sorry. I feel I'm responsible for landing you in this mess, and——"

"Oh, no. It isn't really your fault any more than mine. We've been hopelessly unlucky, that's all."

"You're sure she'll talk?"

"Not a doubt of it. She broadcasts as regularly as the B.B.C. The only hope is that I might persuade Aunt Katherine to come down with me to Miss Pottington's house this afternoon and make a clean breast of it. She pays a certain amount of attention to what Aunt Katherine says."

"It's an idea." Piers looked dissatisfied however.

"Can you think of anything better?"

"No, not really. I was only wondering what you're going to say about the wrong name in the register."

"Oh! I'd forgotten." Nicola stared at him in dismay. And then suddenly he took charge of the situation.

"You'll have to say it was Leigh. That's obvious. It suits your story—and, incidentally, it suits me too. I simply can't have this confounded story following me round—"

"I absolutely refuse," Nicola interrupted firmly. "You can't possibly think so little of me as to imagine that I would saddle your cousin with my indiscretions, too."

"Oh, Nic——"

"Piers, *please* let's keep your cousin out of this."

She saw his mouth harden unexpectedly.

"We won't do anything in a hurry," he said curtly.

"But we'll have to! I've got to give some sort of explanation of my absence. And I'm going to tell the truth—just for a change," she added bitterly.

"Nic, it's so ideal, with Leigh away and everything! If you'll just be brave and determined about your story, the whole thing will be explained and over before he comes home."

"I can't see it like that—Oh, come on, let's get going!"

They paid the bill and set off. The desk clerk had told them there was a garage in the next village; they caught the local bus, found the garage and arranged for the car to be collected and repaired, then set off for the railway station.

Luckily there was a train for Longheedon twenty minutes later, and in another half-hour they had arrived—much to Nicola's relief, for Piers had been remarkably silent during the whole journey.

They left the train still in silence, both very much aware of the jarring note between them.

For her part Nicola felt she would so willingly have helped Piers out of his scrape if she could, for she saw it might indeed have serious consequences for him later. But to involve some entirely innocent person—without even asking his permission! No, that was too——

"Well, I'm damned," Piers said softly beside her. And, looking up in astonishment to see what further complication could have come their way, Nicola saw that a long, familiar black car had just drawn to a standstill in the yard outside the station, and at the wheel sat Leigh Mason.

He saw them at once, and waved to them.

There was nothing to do but go over to him as he got out of the car.

"Why, what on earth are you two doing here?" he asked in surprise.

"We might say the same to you," Piers retorted quickly.

"Hm?—Oh, I came home yesterday evening after all. There'd been some mistake about dates. I'd just run down to the station this morning to get my Sunday paper, without waiting for it to be brought up at lunch-time. But you?" He looked inquiringly from one to the other.

Nicola was not sure what story Piers was going to invent on the spur of the moment, but suddenly she determined that it should not be told. Speaking quickly and a trifle breathlessly, she said:

"Mr. Mason, we're in a rotten scrape——"

"You surprise me." Leigh glanced ironically at his cousin.

"Oh, it isn't Piers's fault. It isn't anyone's fault. Only we simply must get out of it somehow. You see, we went for a drive yesterday evening, and the petrol tank leaked and we were stranded miles from home.

We had to put up for the night at an inn, and this morning, by the most filthy luck, Miss Pottington—the biggest gossip in the village—turned up there, on her way home by car from somewhere or other. I—I tried to bluff——"

"Lie, you mean?"

"Yes, all right, I *didn't* tell her the truth. And then some wretched girl came up and said something terribly unfortunate about 'Mr. Mason'. And now Miss Pottington thinks—Well, you know what she thinks."

"Oh, quite." Leigh Mason looked speculatively at Nicola. "Does your aunt know anything about this?" he asked.

"No." Nicola shook her head. "That's another awful thing. I couldn't get any news through last night."

"Then you'd better let me drive you down there at once. And—yes, this is the best way—I'll do the explaining for you. Mrs. Round will probably attach a little more weight to what I say than to anything Piers could say. I'm sorry, Piers. It certainly does seem a bit of bad luck this time. Will you let me take Miss Round down now and do the explaining? Then I think Mrs. Round herself would be the person to silence Miss Whatever-her-name-is."

"Yes, I thought that," Nicola agreed eagerly.

"It's very good of you, Leigh." Piers spoke slowly. Not exactly reluctantly, but as though he were weighing something up. "If you really don't mind——"

"Of course not. You'd better both get in. I'll drop you at the cross-roads, and take Miss Round on myself."

With a sigh of relief, Nicola got into the car. It

really did seem as though the whole wretched business might smooth out, after all.

A few minutes later the car stopped, and Piers got out.

"Good-bye, Nic. I'm more sorry than I can say. But I hope this is the best way to straighten things out from your point of view."

Nicola smiled as she gave him her hand.

"It is, I'm sure. Don't worry." And she waved her hand to him as Leigh started the car again.

Only then did she remember that the question of the substituted name was still not explained.

"Mr. Mason!" she exclaimed in dismay.

"Yes?" He glanced at her.

"Oh—oh, nothing." How *could* she give Piers away when he himself had chosen to be silent? At the moment Leigh was rather sympathetic towards him. But if he knew this further point, it would be very different.

"Sure there's nothing wrong?" Her employer smiled not unkindly.

"Quite sure. I—I just thought of something, but it's all right, after all."

What on earth was the best thing to do?

If she let things take their course—let Leigh explain to Aunt Katherine—that would be all right up to a point, because neither he nor Aunt Katherine knew anything about the wrong name in the register. The difficulty was always Miss Pottington!

Then the only thing was to take Aunt Katherine into her confidence. Yes—that was it! When Leigh had gone she would tell Aunt Katherine that final unfortunate detail. There *might* be no need to tell Leigh. It was possible that Aunt Katherine would be able to convince Miss Pottington that it was all an unfortunate mistake. One could not imagine Miss Pottington relinquishing such a sensational piece of scandal easily, of course, but—at least there was hope in this way.

The car turned into the drive, and her employer said—again with that not unkindly smile:

"Don't look so worried. No one is going to shoot you."

"No. I know." Nicola laughed a little, but she felt very uncomfortable as she led the way into the hall through the open front door.

At this time in the morning Aunt Katherine was most likely to be in her own little sitting-room, from which she transacted most of her varied business. Nicola went towards the door—and then stopped in petrified dismay.

"But, dear Mrs. Round, I *saw* it—with my own *eyes*!" she heard a high, excited voice exclaim. It could belong to only one person.

Miss Pottington was there before them. Miss Pottington who believed Leigh Mason to be "the man in the case". Miss Pottington who would, no doubt, consider it shameless, but understandable, that he should now turn up with Nicola!

CHAPTER VII

ON the impulse of the moment, and in sheer terror, Nicola caught her employer by the arm, with an intimacy that was quite unusual.

"Well, what is it?" He glanced at her in surprise, not untinged with amusement.

"Don't you hear?" She drew him into the recess made by the angle of the stairs and the passage which led to the kitchen. "It's Miss Pottington! She's here already. That means——" She broke off in dismay at the thought of what it did mean.

"But is that so serious?" He was puzzled and slightly impatient, she saw. "Surely it rather simplifies things. This Miss Pottington has got to be told sometime. We may as well do two explanations in one."

"Oh, you don't understand!" Nicola exclaimed wretchedly.

"I'm afraid I don't."

"Mr. Mason"—she clasped her hands nervously and spoke with rapid earnestness—"it isn't really for me to tell you, but you'll have to know now. Miss Pottington thinks it—it was *you* who were with me at the inn."

"*I*? But why on earth should she think that?"

"Well——" Nicola hesitated and he said sternly:

"You'd better explain, hadn't you?"

"Yes, of course. You see, we—we had to sign some sort of register, and Piers was afraid it might somehow affect his divorce later if anything—came out. And—

and, on the impulse of the moment, he signed your name instead of his own."

"Not, I think, on the impulse of the moment," her employer retorted coldly. And somehow it frightened Nicola that there was nothing at all except that frigid, angry comment.

After a short, uneasy silence, during which he seemed sunk in anything but agreeable thought, she ventured to speak again.

"Well, you see how—awkward it's going to make things."

"I'm busy taking in the implications," he agreed dryly.

"Mr. Mason, you'd better go at once. If she were to see you here with me——"

"Don't be ridiculous. You surely don't imagine that I, too, should back out of this and leave you to face it alone."

"Oh, it hardly matters!"

"Of course it matters."

"I only meant," poor Nicola explained, "that things could hardly be worse, in any case."

"Perfectly true, but an insufficient reason for my leaving you to tackle the unpleasantness singlehanded."

Then, before they could argue the point further, the door of Aunt Katherine's study opened suddenly and Miss Pottington surged into the hall, as though borne on the flood of her own emotions.

"Dear Mrs. Round, I *feel* for you! Indeed I do. With four daughters of your own to consider, you must be *distracted* with worry. This is what comes of letting her go to his house to work at all hours of the day and—I was almost going to say 'night', too. It couldn't possibly come to any—— Oh!"

Like a hen in a farmyard first observing the muzzle of a fox, she stiffened in horror on espying the guilty pair. There was nothing to do but come forward then and, with a coolness which Nicola could only admire, Leigh Mason entered the conversation.

"Miss Pottington, I'm sorry to see you have come here to make scandal and trouble out of a most natural accident. My secretary and I *were* out driving yesterday evening—a perfectly harmless pursuit, you must admit. The car broke down and we were forced to spend the night at the inn where you saw her this morning. I'm afraid her anxiety that you would take —shall we say?—an uncharitable view of the episode prompted her, very foolishly, to tell you a lie. But"— his gaze travelled speculatively over Miss Pottington —"it seems that her estimate of your reaction was not so far wrong, after all."

"Oh, Nicola," Aunt Katherine broke in anxiously, "we've been so terribly worried, child!"

"I know, I know, Aunt Katherine." Nicola caught her aunt's hand in her eagerness. "I tried to telephone, indeed I did. But the phone at this wretched place was out of order."

Miss Pottington sniffed quite audibly. But Aunt Katherine was a match for that sort of comment.

"Telephones are very apt to go wrong," she countered sharply. "If you were on the telephone, my dear, you wouldn't need to be told that." Then, turning from Miss Pottington to Leigh, she continued: "You have no idea how glad I am that Nicola is safe, Mr. Mason. I imagined all sorts of dreadful things had happened. Somehow, I thought she told me it was your cousin, and not you, with whom she was going, and

95

of course he *isn't* such a careful driver as——"

"Dear Mrs. Round, she probably did tell you that!" interrupted Miss Pottington who, in eclipse, was apt to turn acid. "And, now I come to think of it, I did hear, Mr. Mason, that you were going away yesterday until Tuesday morning."

"But, as you see, my plans had to be altered because of what happened." Leigh's tone was pleasantly ironical. "I'm sorry, Miss Pottington, that you're determined to have your little scandal. Are our reputations really to depend upon a breakdown of my car?"

Miss Pottington's indignant gaze wavered—swept the hall—and then finally came to rest upon Leigh's elegant car, standing on the drive outside the open front door.

"A breakdown which, I see, has been most *miraculously* remedied," she observed tartly, "although it is still comparatively early on Sunday morning, when one would expect most garages to be closed."

Nicola had the distinct impression that Leigh had an impulse to murder Miss Pottington at that moment, but he only said coldly:

"That's my other car. We had to leave the smaller one at the inn and come on by train."

"Surely," thought Nicola, "she hasn't got an answer to that one!"

But Miss Pottington, in defence of womanhood in general and that of Longheedon in particular, was not to be daunted.

"There is only one train from Polhaven on Sunday morning, Mr. Mason," she observed with great dignity. "That must have arrived at Longheedon not more than twenty minutes ago. I find it very difficult to see how you and Nicola had time to walk all the way to your house, collect another car, and come down here by this time. But of course, it's no business of *mine*. Not in the very *least*. I am not one to gossip or give censure"—she glared at Nicola—"but when I see very strange things happening which involve the niece of my old friend, Mrs. Round, then duty and not inclination forbids me to keep silent."

"Then duty and not inclination forces me to take the discussion a step further," Leigh retorted curtly, "and tell you that Miss Round and I took a taxi from the station. I hope, Miss Pottington, that you will now be able to fit in your careful timing to the minute."

Miss Pottington turned very red, but, alas! with angry triumph rather than defeat.

"As I have said before, this is not *my* affair," she stated with painful emphasis, "but, dear Mrs. Round, I leave it to *your own good sense* to decide what the truth of this matter is, considering that you know as well as I do that there are no taxis at Longheedon Station on Sundays."

And, very conscious of having had the very, very last word, Miss Pottington made a stately exit—leaving behind her three entirely nonplussed people.

It was Aunt Katherine who spoke first, and for once her tone was not bright and managing. It was perplexed and uncertain.

"I think we'd better go into the study and talk this over *quite* frankly," she said.

"I think we had," agreed Leigh grimly, and they followed Aunt Katherine into the room, Nicola wondering just how furious her employer felt at being involved in this awkward—not to say ridiculous—predicament.

"I suppose he could cheerfully kill us both," she reflected gloomily, "and small blame to him!"

But, if so, he concealed the fact successfully.

Sitting down at her desk, Aunt Katherine took charge of the scene.

"Now, Nicola," she said briskly, "if you've been making a fool of yourself, don't make matters worse by romancing to *me*. It was stupid of you to tell lies to Miss Pottington, but it would be useless to tell them to me. I may as well say at once that, though I was not going to say so in front of Miss Pottington, I most distinctly remember that you did tell me it was Piers Mason with whom you were going out. I think that needs a little explaining."

"Aunt Katherine, I *was* going to tell you the real truth. I wouldn't have told you anything else. We'd decided on that, anyway. I mean, I had——" She glanced apologetically at Leigh, nervous lest he should think she was trying to involve him even more deeply in her concerns.

"*We* decided," he assured her gravely. "You must permit me my share of the decision."

"Thank you. That's—generous of you, Mr. Mason."

Aunt Katherine's eyebrows rose. This hardly sounded like the discussion of an illicit love affair by the two most interested parties.

"Aunt Katherine——" Nicola turned to her aunt again. "It *was* Piers who took me driving yesterday. But it was all quite innocent—do believe that—though terribly unfortunate." And then she explained, with an eager sincerity which carried the unmistakable stamp of truth, just what had happened. She touched as lightly as possible on Piers's subterfuge over the registration of names but, even so, she saw her aunt's eyebrows go up again.

She made no comment, however, and waited with unusual patience until Nicola's somewhat halting story had come to an end. Then Leigh spoke in that formal way of his.

"I must apologize, Mrs. Round, for the part my cousin has played. To do him justice, I am sure he would not willingly have compromised your niece for the world. But that doesn't help us very much now, of course."

"No, it doesn't." Aunt Katherine glanced thoughtfully from one to the other, divided between genuine dismay at the seriousness of the situation and a certain professional pleasure at being presented with an almost insoluble problem.

"You—you do believe me, don't you?" Nicola spoke in almost timid appeal, and Aunt Katherine patted her hand reassuringly.

"Yes, child, I believe you, of course. I'm not so stupid as to suppose I've been deceived about you for two years, and I've lived long enough to know that the obvious explanation is not always the real one. But *my* believing isn't really the important thing at the moment, Nicola. The question is—what are other people going to believe?—especially when Miss Pottington has given the facts as *she* sees them."

"But the matter doesn't concern her in the very least," Leigh exclaimed impatiently, and the grim line of his mouth testified to his acute exasperation. "Isn't there some hope that that in itself will keep her quiet?"

"Not the slightest," Aunt Katherine assured him, evidently thinking Leigh a very simple person if he could really suppose that such a minor consideration would affect the tide of gossip which regularly ebbed and flowed around the foundations of Longheedon's daily life.

"Then you mean that before the week is out, half Longheedon will be imagining that Nicola and I spent the night together at some vulgar wayside inn?"

Aunt Katherine winced slightly. She prided herself on always facing a situation squarely, but this was a particularly unpleasant one.

"It may not be as bad as we expect," she said at last. But her tone was doubtful, and carried no conviction either to herself or her two hearers.

"This is really intolerable!" Leigh sprang to his feet and began pacing up and down Aunt Katherine's study with as much energy as the extremely limited space permitted.

Nicola watched him unhappily for a moment and then said—inadequately, she felt:

"Mr. Mason, I'm terribly sorry——"

But he interrupted her impatiently.

"For heaven's sake, child, don't apologize again. It wasn't your fault—except for the initial stupidity of running around with anyone like Piers."

Nicola relapsed abruptly into silence, at least as much annoyed by this lofty vindication as she could have been by any form of blame. Characteristically Leigh appeared to be supremely aware of her anger.

"One thing is quite clear——" He paused beside Nicola's chair and regarded her with a look of concentration which suggested that his thoughts were not at all on her, but on the words he was carefully weighing at the moment. "We must stick to the story that it *was* I who was with you. I——"

"Oh, but it's so terribly unfair!" Nicola protested. "It's bad enough to have my own reputation ruined, but to have you dragged in, when you weren't even within miles of that wretched inn, is too bad."

"That can't be helped." He was curt and to the point. "I can see no reason to depart from the truth in any other particular when we are telling our version of the story. But if we start elaborating the theme with people impersonating each other it will be useless to expect the most charitable person to believe us."

Nicola looked at him in distressed silence. What he said was quite true, of course, but her sense of fairness made it a most unwelcome business. As though her objections were all disposed of, in any case, Leigh went on without giving her time to speak.

"The simple outline is that you went out with me, the car broke down and we had to put up at the nearest inn for the night. We must stick to that in face of any scepticism. A calm insistence on the part of all three of us is bound to have its effect in the end."

"Yes." Nicola's face brightened. "Perhaps you're right. We'll take every opportunity of speaking of the matter, with no attempt at concealment or—or embarrassment. At least"—she made a little face—"we must try not to be embarrassed. As you say, if we treat it in a perfectly matter-of-fact way, as though we simply don't expect people to believe us, they *must* be impressed in the end. Don't you think that's the best way, Aunt Katherine?"

"Yes, that's quite all right. In any case, we must

make the best of it now, and certainly I will use any weight I have in Longheedon to support your story."

There didn't seem to be much more to discuss after that. Leigh picked up his hat, shook hands with Aunt Katherine and then turned to Nicola once more.

"Good-bye, Miss Round." They had become secretary and employer once more, she noticed. "I hope we can get you out of this unpleasant business without too much painful publicity. I am extremely sorry about it all."

"*You* don't have to apologize any more either," Nicola told him crossly, still smarting a little under what he had said to her. Then, as she saw the slightly amused lift of his eyebrows, she said rather more meekly: "Do you want me to come as usual to-morrow?"

"Why, of course. We have to behave exactly as though nothing has happened, remember. To break off your employment with me now would be the worst possible sign."

"Yes, of course. I just thought you—you might be so sick of the whole business——" Nicola broke off unhappily.

But if she expected kindly reassurance from her employer she was disappointed. All he said was:

"We can't either of us afford to be sick of the whole business at the moment."

Then he said good-bye and took his leave.

It was not until lunch-time that Nicola met the family in full force, and then the varying reactions of her cousins supplied some indication of what she might expect from people in general.

Bridget and Caroline both took the view that it

was terribly silly of her to have contrived to get herself involved in such a scrape. Neither of them appeared inclined to consider the circumstances on their own merits. They simply thought these things should not be allowed to happen. If they did, it was a proof of some sort of silly inefficiency on the part of the person to whom they happened.

Diana, more tolerant than her sisters—and possibly conscious of the fact that it was the sort of scrape in which she herself might well have been involved—simply said:

"Poor old Nic! Rough luck. All the unpleasantness of losing your reputation and none of the fun of it. But I bet your woe and fury is nothing compared to the feelings of that starchy Leigh Mason. The most astonishing bit to me is how you ever persuaded him to take you out in the first place."

"Diana, you talk with less sense of responsibility than a child," exclaimed Anne disgustedly. "You don't seem to realize that Nicola has thrown away her good name with both hands."

"And you don't seem to realize, Anne, that the whole thing was an accident!" Nicola retorted, pale with anger. "Or are we to understand that you prefer to think badly of me, rather than accept my story?"

Anne was slightly taken aback, but she only shrugged and said:

"You've been larking about with both those Masons for long enough. It was bound to come to something like this in the end."

Nicola was rendered speechless for a moment by both fury and amusement that anyone should describe her very distant relations with Leigh Mason as "larking about". But afterwards, when she went over the scene again to herself in her own room, she was aware of a chilled dismay. If at least one in her own family circle was willing to judge her unfairly, and two unsympathetically, how was she going to face with uncharitable acquaintances?

To be sure, Anne's attitude was dictated by a certain annoyed jealousy because her cousin and not she, had occupied whatever limelight there had been in connection with the two Masons when they first came to Longheedon. But if Anne could act from unworthy motives, why not others too?

The afternoon dragged away with a measured slowness which somehow suggested that one was waiting for something to happen. "Like waiting for a verdict," thought poor Nicola. "And I suppose that's more or less what it *is*. Though goodness knows just when the village will choose to pronounce its verdict."

She rather thought that Piers might put in an appearance about tea-time, but either caution or an uncomfortable sense of guilt kept him away. She tried not to think harshly of him, for she, least of anyone, should judge hastily just now. But the plain fact was that Piers didn't come well out of this business.

One could allow for some natural anxiety about his own peculiar position, and it was inevitable that he should act with a view to making the way clear for his divorce later. But, whatever the excuse, he had behaved very badly where Leigh was concerned, and not very creditably where she herself was concerned, come to that.

"Oh, it's easy to be wise now," Nicola told herself impatiently, but she knew that one of the most unhappy features of the whole episode was that Piers had acted in a way which made her feel more than a little disappointed in him.

After tea Aunt Katherine said:

"Who is coming to church? You will, of course, Nicola, and——"

"Oh, Aunt Katherine, not just to-day, of all days!"

"Yes, certainly. Specially to-day, of all days," Aunt Katherine retorted briskly. "Don't you see, you silly child, that it is essential you should appear in public as much—and as calmly—as possible?"

Nicola saw the force of this, while dreading the necessity of putting it into action. But when Diana, rather unexpectedly, offered to come too, she felt she must certainly show a little courage, and she agreed to come.

She thought it was quite the most difficult thing she had ever done, particularly as Aunt Katherine was, as usual, delayed until the very last moment by half a dozen unexpected duties, and so they arrived only just as the service was about to begin.

The church was unusually full—or so it seemed to Nicola's uneasy first glance—and it took all the resolution she had to walk calmly down the aisle beside Diana, while Aunt Katherine (really a tower of strength in this emergency) dispensed her usual gracious smiles, as though quite unaware that, in one or two pews, hats or bonnets were pushed close together and sibilant whispers were exchanged.

By a supreme effort, Nicola contrived to keep her gaze from faltering, but she was badly shaken when she found that the first person whose glance she met directly turned out to be Miss Pottington.

It was Miss Pottington's gaze which shifted first, but not from any sense of confusion, Nicola saw. Instinctively, her own eyes turned in the same direction, and it was with difficulty that she suppressed a gasp.

In a pew near the front, on the other side of the aisle, sat Leigh Mason, looking for all the world as though he had no other thought than to take a grave and considered pleasure in Evensong that Sunday evening.

As Nicola looked at him, he seemed to become aware of her and, with a perfection of manner which she could only admire, he gave her the authentic bow of the employer to his secretary. Pleasant, gracious, but distinctively remote.

Nicola could really have hugged him for it.

She could have hugged him for coming to church at all, as a matter of fact, for she knew it had been deliberately arranged on her behalf. He evidently guessed that such a good general as Aunt Katherine would hardly let such an opportunity pass, and he accordingly arranged to be there, to second her gallant efforts.

As they took their places, Diana contrived to whisper:

"Good work!"

Nicola smiled faintly in reply, and for a moment her spirits soared.

Then from the next pew came a particularly piercing whisper. Old Mrs. Oakley was speaking to her sister and, being slightly deaf herself, she usually concluded that everyone else was, too.

"Absolutely brazen," she hissed. "Just as Miss P. said. In church, too! They'd do better to come here

106

together instead of separately—*and* not to Evensong either."

"Ssh," returned her sister, quivering with interest. "Here comes the dear Vicar."

CHAPTER VIII

NICOLA heard very little of the service that evening, and more than once she was very near tears.

She told herself again and again that she imagined at least half of the interested, unfriendly glances which seemed to be directed at her—and no doubt that was true—but even so, she felt that what Miss Pottington would doubtless call "the finger of scorn" was being pointed at her.

"It's ridiculous to feel like this when I've done nothing wrong," Nicola thought angrily. And then—"Oh, but why did I lie to Miss Pottington? That *was* wrong and silly, of course, and perhaps all the trouble came from that. Only, would she have believed me, whatever I had said?"

The answer was undoubtedly: "No."

Once she glanced surreptitiously across the aisle, to see how her employer was taking this experience. If he felt as uncomfortable and miserable as she did, he did it admirably, and she could only hope that she was concealing her feelings as well.

It was over at last. People were moving slowly out of the church, like a broad, leisurely stream, and here and there were eddies and cross-currents where parties converged to exchange the news of the week, or inquire after each other's health.

Just outside the porch Leigh caught up with the Round family and greeted them affably, while one or two people near fell strangely silent.

"Good evening, Mrs. Round. Good evening, Miss

Round. I hope you have got over your tiresome experience."

"Oh, yes, thank you, _I_ have, but—" Nicola spoke clearly and a little viciously—"I think some other people haven't. It's astonishing how many people try to make scandal out of nothing."

"Oh—do you think so?" Leigh looked vaguely surprised. "Only those with nasty minds, I think—or perhaps with little intelligence."

Conversation round them was taken up again rather quickly, but Nicola noticed that, as they moved off, some very unfriendly glances followed them.

"You're awfully good at this sort of thing," Diana told him, when they were out of earshot of the rest of the congregation. "It isn't long practice, I suppose?"

"Diana! Please behave yourself," Aunt Katherine said sharply.

But Leigh looked amused, rather than affronted.

"I have contrived to steer clear of compromising situations up to the present," he assured her. "But then—" and, if Nicola had not known his grave disposition so well, she would have thought his eyes twinkled—"but then I have always had a man for my secretary until now."

"Oh, don't you try to put it on to Nic," Diana said, with a casual loyalty that was rather attractive. "She's as good as gold. And even if you'd compromised her to the extent of having to marry her—I can think of a lot more unpleasant things that could happen to a man than that."

"Di—please!" Nicola thought she could have done without that kind of championship.

Perhaps Leigh thought so too, because he didn't

take up the subject. And a moment or two later he said good night to them all, and turned off from the road to walk across the fields.

"Diana, you shouldn't have said that!" Nicola protested, as soon as they were alone. "The situation's embarrassing enough without your contributing that sort of remark."

"I was only ragging him," Diana said placidly. "You shouldn't take things so seriously. And nor should he, come to that. You both behave as though the fate of nations were in the balance. After all, even if you *had* spent the night with him——"

"Diana!" Her mother spoke with angry sharpness. "You are *not* to say things like that. You're worse than Edward at times. Quite as irresponsible, and quite—quite——"

"—As uncannily accurate," suggested Diana without heat.

"I am extremely displeased with you," Aunt Katherine told her sharply. But Diana seemed entirely unmoved by this fact and the walk home was completed in slightly strained silence.

The next week was probably the unhappiest—and certainly the most agitating—that Nicola had ever spent.

At one time she would have innocently enjoyed a little notice from people. Now all she asked was that no head should turn as she passed, on comment be whispered, and even no one's thoughts be occupied by the subject of her unworthy self.

Undoubtedly, she imagined some of the glances and comments. But, even allowing for that, it was obvious that Miss Pottington's original story—startling enough in itself—had received some picturesque additions in the re-telling.

It was amazing how much of the story—in snatches—came back to one or other of the Round family. From spite, from anxiety, from genuine friendliness or from sheer curiosity, almost all their friends and acquaintances contrived to mention the incident. And Nicola was well aware that three, at least, of her cousins were furious about it.

It was specially unfortunate, of course, that Leigh was practically a stranger in the district, and therefore doubly suspect.

"*And* a writer," as Miss Pottington said. "We all know how lax *they* can be. Look at Byron! Look at Oscar Wilde!"

Those who knew anything about either Byron or Oscar Wilde duly looked at them, and found their private lives singularly unreassuring.

It certainly made one think.

Someone said at this point that ought not the Vicar to be told about it all?

But Miss Pottington, who had received remarkably short shrift at the hands of the Vicar, when she had tried to interest him in her story, hastily demurred.

"The dear Vicar is very, very unworldly," she asserted, quite incorrectly. "To the pure all things *are* pure, you know. I'm afraid he wouldn't understand our point of view at all."

"Couldn't poor Mrs. Round make him marry her?" inquired someone, rather ambiguously.

"I hope—indeed I do hope—that will be the final solution," Miss Pottington agreed. "But one never knows, with these shameless people who call themselves modern."

Meanwhile Nicola—who certainly would never have "called herself modern"—continued to go daily to Thorpe Compton as in the past. But her pleasure in her work was spoilt.

So also was her pleasure in her friendship with Piers. It was not only that she felt he had behaved badly. *He* was uneasily aware of it too, and the frank, carefree relationship which had existed between them had suddenly become impossible.

It was true that he made some attempt to justify himself, but Nicola felt she would have preferred him to leave the subject alone.

"I'm afraid you must be feeling very sore and angry with me," was what he said, the first time he was able to speak to her alone.

"No, Piers, it's all right." Nicola, aware that he was once more breaking the rule against coming into her office while she was working, wished profoundly that he would go away.

"But I must have a word with you about this wretched business," he protested. "You do know, don't you, that I wouldn't have involved you in this for anything in the world, if I could have helped it?"

"Yes, I know. It just can't be helped."

"But you feel I ought to have done *something* about it?" he pressed.

"No."

"Then why won't you smile at me?"

"I don't feel much like smiling, Piers. And please go away. You know your cousin doesn't like you to come in here while I'm working."

"Oh, Leigh! I believe it's he who has set you against me."

"No one has set me against you. And it isn't very generous of you to talk disparagingly of your cousin just now. You have nothing against him. If anything, the shoe is on the other foot, you know."

"Good lord! Is it because of *Leigh* that you look so solemnly at me? But, darling——"

"Please don't. It isn't for me to criticize your behaviour to your cousin. But, if you want to know, I think you behaved abominably where he is concerned. You've involved him in a perfectly rotten position, and now you talk quite airily about it, as though you yourself had a grievance, if anyone has."

"But, Nic dear, no one can look after himself better than Leigh can! You really don't have to waste a lot of pity on him. I know it was very cool of me to take his name in vain like that but, hang it all! he's got the sort of reputation that can stand a squib or two, while——"

"I think you're a little too sure of that," Nicola retorted sharply. "In a hotbed of gossip like this some very nasty things can be said—and *are* being said. Probably people are being even more uncharitable about him than they are about me. And that's saying something," she added with a sigh.

"I'm sorry, Nic. Indeed I'm sorry—about old Leigh as well as about you. But you *must* understand, dear, that I simply *had* to do something like that. I simply couldn't afford to get mixed up in a scandal myself, whereas Leigh has absolutely no one but himself to consider. It's unpleasant, I know—but nothing like so unpleasant for him as it is for you. It never is so rotten for the man. And people forget quite quickly and——"

113

"I think," Nicola said rather coldly, "that you under-estimate Longheedon's length of memory. The kind of people who have enough time and ill-nature to go around telling each other that he ought to make an honest woman of me will always have enough time and ill-nature to remember this story against him."

"I say! Is that really what they're saying?—That Leigh ought to marry you?"

"I suppose so. It's the kind of idiotic Victorian theory Miss Pottington and her kind would have."

"How frightful!"

"Yes. It's pretty dense and—and uncharitable of them."

"I think," Nicola said, "that we've talked all this over long enough. And really I've a lot of work to do."

"All right. I'm going. But, Nic—" he came a step nearer and spoke eagerly—"you do understand my point, don't you? You do see that I couldn't do anything but what I did?"

"I see you think so," Nicola said. "I'm sure you honestly believe it. Let's leave it at that, shall we?"

"But you don't agree with me?"

"Piers, I hope I shouldn't have done the same thing in similar circumstances. I don't want to presume to judge you, and of course no one knows just what they will do in a given case, until the time comes along. But I don't like what you did—I'm not going to pretend I do—and, as I say, I hope I shouldn't have done such a thing myself. That's all."

"Well, it's a good deal," Piers said, flushing slightly. He was considerably annoyed, she could see, but perhaps even he felt that he could hardly improve the situation by further discussion, and presently he left her.

Later her employer came in, and he, too, seemed in anything but an amiable mood. Nicola could not decide whether it was because of anything to do with herself or not, but it made her feel very disconsolate, and she thought forlornly how completely life had managed to change in the last week or ten days. Everything had seemed good fun and full of promise before, and now: "People are cross about nothing, and I feel pretty bad-tempered myself," was how Nicola put it to herself.

It might be not "nothing", of course, which was making Leigh Mason look grim and preoccupied and, just as she was preparing to go that afternoon, she saw him glance at her speculatively, as though there were something he wanted to say but he was not quite sure of the wisdom of saying it.

"Did you want something, Mr. Mason?" Nicola looked at him inquiringly.

"Well, yes, as a matter of fact, I did."

He got up, thrusting his hands into his pockets in that way which always suggested slight nervousness, in spite of his general air of imperturbability. "I wanted to ask you just how this business is affecting you. We've already given the—the air of stolid innocence something of a trial. I wondered whether you felt happy about the result."

Nicola slowly put down her gloves and handbag on the desk again.

"Well, I don't know that 'happy' is quite the word," she admitted.

"No? Why not exactly?"

"Well, for one thing, it doesn't seem to have worked very well," Nicola said bluntly. "I mean—people are talking just the same, aren't they?"

"You're finding that too? I supposed so. My dear, what are we going to do about it?"

It struck her for the first time that he was not only looking his age, but tired and even a little dispirited too.

"Oh, don't worry," Nicola reassured him hastily. "It will blow over. It's bound to in the end. And there isn't anything we *can* do about it, is there?"

"I'm not sure that I agree with you there." He frowned thoughtfully. "And I certainly don't agree about the whole thing blowing over. This damned story is going to stick to you indefinitely, you know.'

"And you too, I suppose," Nicola admitted ruefully.

"Oh, it doesn't matter so much for me. It never does matter so much for the man," he added, as Piers had. "But for you——" he broke off, and then, as though finally making up his mind, he turned from the window where he had been standing. "Nicola, do you mind telling me if there is anyone you're very fond of?"

"A man, you mean?"

"Of course."

"Well—no. That is, I'm not engaged or—or thinking of it, if that's what you want to know."

She felt confused, wondering how much he had guessed of her feeling for Piers. Or, if so, whether he also guessed that perhaps this had undergone something of a change. She glanced doubtfully at him.

"Why do you want to know, Mr. Mason?"

"Because," he said, apparently coming out of rather deep thought, "there is one crude but simple solution to this business. If you married me——".

"*Married* you?" gasped Nicola.

116

"Exactly." His rather unkind smile reminded Nicola very much of their first encounter. "I quite understand that the remedy may seem worse than the evil, but I offer the suggestion for what it is worth."

"Oh, I—didn't mean that, exactly." Nicola had recovered herself slightly. "I only meant—" she paused and then finished lamely—"I couldn't imagine you married to anyone."

"Believe me, Nicola," he said dryly, "I've never been able to imagine it either."

"You'd just hate it, wouldn't you?" she said frankly.

"Being married to you?"

"Being married to anyone."

He smiled slightly.

"As your cousin said—I suppose there are many more unpleasant things that could happen to a man."

"Oh—Di! Did she put this ridiculous—I mean, this idea into your head?"

"Come, I'm not dependent on people like—Di, for my ideas." And then, as she laughed, he added: "I'm really quite serious about this, you know."

"But, Mr. Mason, I don't think you even like me very much," Nicola protested.

"On the contrary, I think you're charming," he assured her a little formally.

"I don't think that's quite enough to marry on, do you?" Nicola smiled and picked up her gloves and bag again.

"In the ordinary way, of course not. But this wretched business has reached very serious proportions. It's ridiculous, I agree. It's also infuriating. But that doesn't alter the situation. Our names are what is popularly described as 'mud' in this confounded place,

117

and there seems precious little chance of the matter righting itself by our just sitting down and looking innocent."

Nicola regarded him in troubled silence for a moment. What he said was quite true, of course, and, in the last day or two, she had been realizing how much her unfortunate adventure was affecting even the other members of the family. Scandal, in a place like Longheedon, was so very much a mushroom growth. Before you knew where you were it had assumed enormous proportions. Suppose she rewarded all that Aunt Katherine and her family had done for her by tarnishing their bright position in the little world they all enjoyed so much.

Then, before she could decide what to say, her employer spoke again.

"I don't want to sound like a man who thinks that marriage is the first step towards the divorce court, but—if we considered this rather fantastic remedy at all—it would be clearly understood, of course, that it was hardly the regulation marriage, and that we—well, we need not regard it as permanent. I'm much too old for you, for one thing," he added irrelevantly, as though the idea had just struck him.

"Are you?" Nicola suppressed a certain natural curiosity with difficulty. "I think it's awfully nice of you to put it so reassuringly—and actually to be willing to mess up your own life in order to get me out of this scrape. But I don't think——"

"No—wait a moment." He stopped her with a smile. "Don't decide in a hurry. After all, the idea has only just been presented to you, and"—the smile became rather dry—"I gather it was a good deal of shock.

Think it over—see what happens in the next few days. But remember, if you do feel that—marrying me is the best solution, I should take good care of you—" ("Does he think I'm a baby?" thought Nicola)—"and you should do more or less as you liked here. I'm not exactly a wealthy man—I suppose no one is in these days—but I think I could promise you most things that you want."

"With the—the definite idea that the marriage didn't last, for ever, and that it was—was——"

"Only a matter of form, in any case?" he suggested.

Nicola nodded.

"My dear, you should have your divorce whenever it could suitably be arranged. And, as for the other, I can only remind you that I've been a bachelor by choice for a good many years now, and I'm much more likely to err on the side of treating you as a secretary, rather than as a wife."

Nicola smiled.

"Could I go on being your secretary?"

"I should be charmed," he assured her. "You're shaping well as a secretary. I shouldn't really like to lose you."

Nicola drew a deep breath.

On the surface, the idea was fantastic, of course. And yet the very thought of escaping from the problems which had been hemming her in was a relief. She knew there was nothing like a wedding for silencing the conventional-minded people of Longheedon. Even Miss Pottington considered that orange-blossom covered a multitude of sins quite adequately.

"Well, go along home now." Her employer spoke as though a somewhat minor matter had been more or less settled. "Think it over, and tell me what you decide."

"Thank you. I—Do you mind if I discuss it with Aunt Katherine?"

"Not at all," he said—but rather stiffly, so that she wondered if he very much hated his private affairs being talked over like this.

Perhaps, after all, it was something she would settle for herself. And, on that, she said good-bye to him, and set off for home.

On the way, she tried to look at this offer of his in a different light. Not only from the point of view of a means of rescue from her present position, but on its own merits.

Seriously, what *would* it be like to live in the same house as Leigh Mason?— as his wife, in fact, however much they chose to disregard the position. Come to that, did she really like him or didn't she? Did his uprightness, his unexpected kindness, his undoubted charm, outweigh the fact that he was a reserved and sarcastic man, with very little of the softer outlook on life in his composition?

It was no wonder Nicola's face wore an extremely preoccupied expression as she walked home across the fields.

When she came out on the main road, at the foot of the long hill leading up to Aunt Katherine's house, Anne came abreast of her. She could hardly do other than walk up the hill beside Nicola, but conversation was decidedly strained and difficult, for the little the two cousins had ever had in common had disappeared under the strain of the last week or two.

It was perhaps in sheer desperation at the silence,

or perhaps because she genuinely thought her more resourceful cousin might have some suggestion to make that Nicola suddenly said:

"Anne, can *you* think of any way to stop all this wretched gossip and scandal?"

"Yes." Anne spoke in that positive way of hers that allowed of little argument. "There are two ways: You could go away and get a job somewhere else——"

"Anne!"

"—Or Leigh Mason could marry you."

"Do you—do you really think that would be a solution?" Nicola spoke in a low voice.

"Which—the marrying? Yes, that would probably be the best solution from his point of view."

"From *his* point of view?"

"Of course. Were you thinking only of yourself?" Anne inquired with infuriating superiority.

"N-no. Only I hadn't thought of the problem being sufficiently pressing for *him* to need such a remedy."

"Hadn't you? Do you suppose it's particularly good for him to have a 'seduction of a village maiden' story tagging after him? These things get round, you know, when they happen to be about anyone with any sort of name. I believe it's already had unfortunate results for him."

"What do you *mean*?"

Anne shrugged.

"I don't know that there's any point in discussing it."

"Of course there is. I've a right to know."

"Well then, I know for a fact that he was going to apply for some special job in connection with this Government work of his. A sort of semi-political, semisocial job that would have entailed trips to America and generally representing authority a good deal higher than himself. Sir Charles advised him not to apply for it until this business has blown over because——"

"But it's ridiculous!" exclaimed Nicola. "I simply don't believe that government circles—or any other circles, come to that—are so naïve as to turn down a suitable man simply because there's a little scandal attaching to him."

"No, of course not. But when there are several people of more or less equal merit, they don't choose one whose previous record suggests he might complicate things at the wrong moment by some gross indiscretion."

Nicola stopped dead, forcing Anne to do the same.

"Anne—is that true?"

"Certainly. You must be rather simple, Nic, if you can't see it for yourself."

"So that this hateful business might well spoil the work he enjoys so much?"

Anne shrugged again—a gesture which she favoured since it implied a certain superiority.

"You might both have thought of that before, if I may say so."

But Nicola was too deep in thought even to be angry.

"Please tell Aunt Katherine not to keep tea for me," she said with sudden decision. "I'll be a bit late. I'm going back to Thorpe Compton now."

"All that way?" Anne looked surprised. "Have you forgotten something? Surely to-morrow will do."

"No," Nicola said. "To-morrow won't do. And I haven't forgotten anything. I'm going back to tell Leigh Mason that I'll marry him."

CHAPTER IX

"But, my dear"—Leigh Mason leant back in his chair and regarded his breathless secretary with a good deal of astonishment—"why this sudden decision? It is less than half an hour since you left here, anything but in favour of the idea, if I'm not much mistaken."

"Yes. I know." Nicola, who had run a good part of the way back across the fields, had some difficulty in finding her words. "I know, but—that is, I wasn't *against* the idea. Only I hadn't made up my mind. And then I met someone——"

"Who?"

"Does that matter?"

"Well, yes, I think it does. After all"—that faintly sardonic smile appeared—"as your future husband, I might be allowed a certain curiosity about the person who made up your mind, don't you think?"

"Oh, *she* didn't make up my mind."

"She?"

"It was Anne. My cousin, you know."

"Oh, yes. And she said——?"

"She spoke about—the general scandal. The way it was affecting—both of us. I suppose, too,- she was thinking how unpleasant it is for all of *them*. Because it is, you know. And then she, too, said something about one solution being for—for us to marry. And then suddenly I saw it as the only way out."

"A desperate remedy, in fact." Leigh smiled slightly as he got up and came round to the other side of the desk. He took her hand lightly, and looked down

123

at her with something very serious in his expression. "My dear, I'm so sorry you're being thrust into this. It's quite wrong, of course, that your young life should be moulded by force in this way. But, frankly, I don't know what else we're to do. I can only tell you that I—well, I'll do my best to make it as bearable as possible and——"

"*I'll* do my best too," Nicola explained eagerly. "I don't imagine it's very nice for *you* to have to think of having something young and frivolous and—and rather silly around all the time."

"Being so very far removed from anything young and frivolous myself." He smiled dryly, but he touched her cheek with rather gentle fingers, and Nicola found suddenly that she very much liked the feel of his hand.

"I didn't mean quite that, you know."

"I know. It's unkind to tease you. You're a good child." He said that with a slight sigh, as though the fact laid some sort of responsibility upon him.

Nicola smiled mischievously.

"You didn't want me to be anything else, did you?"

"Of course not."

"You sounded a bit as though it worried you."

"Oh, we-ell"—he actually put his arm round her as he came with her to the door—"it makes you rather more of a responsibility, you know."

"But do you have to look on me as *your* responsibility?"

"If I marry you—of course."

"Even in the circumstances?"

"It will be my business to look after you, naturally. I don't know who else should."

"It doesn't strike you that I might be quite well able to look after myself?"

"No, Nicola. I can't say it ever struck me that way at all," he said with a smile. "But I'll try not to be too much the heavy husband."

Nicola looked up suddenly and smiled in her turn.

"May I say something awfully personal?"

"I should imagine this is the very moment for saying it," he said gravely, but his eyes sparkled amusedly.

"Well then, I think you will make an extraordinarily nice husband."

"My dear, that's really very generous of you." A little to her surprise, he actually flushed slightly. "I don't know that I've ever given you any reason to think that of me. In fact, I was afraid that being my secretary might have given you the reverse impression."

On a sudden impulse, Nicola slipped her arm into his.

"You know, you and Piers are rather absurd, the way you insist on keeping up this fiction that you're a difficult person. As a matter of fact——"

"I seem to remember that you also subscribed to this same absurd fiction once," he reminded her thoughtfully.

"Oh, but I got over it!"

"Entirely?"

"Well——"

He laughed and patted the hand which was resting on his arm.

"Well, we won't press that too far. I'm glad if you feel fairly—confident. A little wholesome awe from one's secretary is one thing, but from one's wife——"

He paused, his eyes widening slightly as he looked at her, and Nicola felt certain that, for the first time, he suddenly saw her *as* his wife.

After a moment he said, with characteristic abruptness:

"Shall I come over with you now and explain to your aunt?"

"Oh—no, thank you. It's all right. I'll explain." Nicola had an idea that she might find it easier to make explanations in her own way, rather than stand by while someone else made them.

"You're sure?"

"Yes. But would you like to come over and see her later this evening? I suppose you would *have* to see her, anyway."

"Undoubtedly. She is your guardian, isn't she?"

"More or less—yes."

"Will after dinner this evening do? I have a dinner engagement, but of course I could——"

"Oh, yes. That would do splendidly. And, Mr. Mason——"

"I'm afraid it really will have to be Leigh in future," he pointed out gravely.

"Of course!" She laughed, but she flushed, too, as she said his name. "Well then—Leigh—will you tell Piers, or—or shall I?"

She wished his expression would not harden in that slight but unmistakable manner.

"There won't be any need for either of us to tell him, for the moment. Piers was called away suddenly on business this afternoon. He won't be back for some time."

"Some time!" She was startled and made no attempt

to hide the fact. "It seems very sudden."

"It was very sudden," Leigh agreed. And that seemed all there was to say about it.

There was a short pause. Then she said:

"Well then, I shall see you this evening."

"Yes. And—thank you, Nicola."

"For what?" She smiled a little.

"Oh—for finding me just bearable," he said lightly.

Aunt Katherine accepted the announcement with something between dismay, lest her niece should not be doing the best thing for her happiness, and pleasure at being faced by the exhilarating difficulties of having to arrange a wedding at such short notice.

"Because it *will* have to be at short notice, of course, Nicola dear. That is to say, not at *too* short notice," she added, on second thoughts, "or people will talk more than ever, if you know what I mean."

Nicola said she knew exactly what her aunt meant.

The rest of the family accepted the news with the amiable indifference which characterized nearly all their reactions to anything which did not concern themselves personally.

"Well, that really does seem the best solution," was Bridget's perfectly well-meaning comment.

"I suppose he's quite rich, isn't he, Nic?' said Diana. "Start by asking plenty, because a man often gets meaner as he goes on, but very seldom more generous. At least—not towards his wife, I mean," she added thoughtfully.

"Di, you're nothing but a gold-digger," exclaimed Anne disgustedly.

Diana shrugged good-humouredly.

"I'd rather be cheerful and grasping than grizzle virtuously on a short allowance," she asserted with candour. "And frankly, I think most men would rather pay up and have their wives satisfied than live perpetually with an economical misery. Only, of course, most of them don't ever face that fact."

"That will do, girls." Aunt Katherine was sometimes astonished to find what shocking things her dumb Diana could suddenly give vent to.

"Anyway, I should think Leigh would be on the generous side," commented Caroline. "You're an exceedingly fortunate girl, Nic."

Nicola accepted this as gracefully as she could, not quite sure whether her cousin meant she had made a lucky escape from a very doubtful position, or whether it was merely Caroline's way of offering conventional congratulations.

It was Anne who asked:

"And is Leigh very much the happy fiancé?"

"If you must know—*yes!*" retorted Nicola angrily. And she suddenly thought: "Oh, I wish he'd pretend to be madly in love with me—at any rate while Anne is around."

Really, one didn't want to be unthankful for small mercies but, after all, it was not exactly elevating to one's pride to be married just for the sake of silencing gossip.

With some such thought in her mind, Nicola slipped away immediately after dinner, pulled a coat over her light dress, and set off down the hill with the intention of meeting Leigh, rather than having to greet him in front of the family.

"We haven't even arranged yet if he shall kiss me

in public," she thought worriedly. And when she saw him coming through the gate on to the road, she felt all the problems of her position suddenly weigh upon her.

Well, at any rate, he was walking, which meant they would have more time to discuss things than if he had had the car.

He greeted her smilingly, but was evidently slightly surprised that she should have walked down to meet him.

"This doesn't mean that anything has gone wrong, I hope?" He took her arm—quite casually, as though he were used to doing so—as they turned to stroll back up the hill together.

"Oh, no. No, not at all," Nicola hastened to assure him. "It's only that—well, we haven't arranged quite everything, have we?"

"Haven't we? What else have we left to arrange?"

Nicola didn't find the answer to this immediately, and she saw that, as usual, he was faintly amused by her confusion.

"Leigh——"

"Yes, my dear."

"Could you—could you manage to appear very— fond of me?"

"Without the slightest difficulty."

"No—I mean seriously."

"So do I," he assured her, although he was smiling. "Do you think you are such a difficult person for one to be fond of?"

"N-no, I suppose not."

"Oh—I see. You thought the difficulty would be for me to express it?"

"Well——" Nicola hesitated. "Leigh, I know it sounds petty and—and small, but I do so hate Anne —I mean, everyone—thinking so positively that I'm just being married because I got myself into a scrape. Being married to save one's face is only a degree better than being married to save one's respectability. It's—it's rather humiliating."

He coolly transferred his arm to her waist with a practised skill she would not have expected.

"You mean—will I do my best to appear madly in love with you?" he said gravely.

"Well——"

"Darling——" He bent his head and lightly kissed the side of her cheek. "I'll do my damnedest."

"Oh——" began Nicola, a good deal startled by the kiss, but a great deal more so by the "darling".

"But you will have to take it better than that, you know," he assured her. "You looked as though I were the last person on earth you expected to kiss you."

"Well, you are," Nicola said before she could stop herself.

He looked a good deal amused.

"I seem to be considerably better at this sort of thing than you, Nicola. I think *you* are the one who needs the practice."

Nicola looked at him suspiciously.

"Are you," she inquired, "by any chance, laughing at me?"

"A little. Do you mind?"

"No," Nicola admitted. "No, I suppose I don't."

"In fact—think how much more perturbing it would be if I kissed you and called you charming names in all seriousness," he pointed out.

Nicola didn't answer that, and after a moment he said:

"Then it's settled that I make discreet love to you in front of people—particularly Anne?"

She laughed then and drew a little against him.

"Leigh, you're very nice."

He didn't ask her why she said that just then, but his arm tightened with an unexpected warmth, and Nicola suddenly felt certain that he would put up a very good show in front of Anne—or, indeed, in front of anyone else.

When they came into the house, they found the whole family assembled in the lounge, drawn there by a variety of reasons, ranging from a sense of duty to frank curiosity—and, in Edward's case, maternal compulsion. This probably accounted for his slightly ferocious air of boredom.

It was rather a trying moment, Nicola thought, this entry under the combined interested gaze of the family. But Leigh seemed completely unruffled by it.

He shook hands with Aunt Katherine and said:

"I hear Nicola has already told you she has promised to marry me."

"Yes." Aunt Katherine's expression hovered between worry and congratulation. "Yes, indeed, I do hope this is the right thing to do."

"Don't be silly, Mother!" exclaimed Anne, before anyone else could say anything. "You know that in the circumstances it's much the best thing to do."

"There is no need to qualify that." There was a certain steely quality in the pleasant smile which Leigh gave Anne. "In any circumstances it would be the best thing, in my eyes."

Anne was slightly taken aback, Nicola saw. However, she contented herself with the faintly deprecating shrug which she evidently thought fitted the occasion. Presumably she meant that she would *dream* of disputing the assertion, but wasn't it asking one to be rather credulous?

"I think," Leigh said slowly, looking round at them all, "that, at any rate in the family circle, we'd better get this straight. Naturally you all think I'm marrying Nicola in order to silence the general gossip. As a matter of fact, you're quite wrong." Putting an arm round Nicola, he drew her against him with an air of indulgent fondness which made it difficult for her not to voice her congratulation aloud. "I'm marrying Nicola because I love her and because she is good enough to think I can make her happy, even though"—he smiled slightly—"I'm rather too old for her."

There was a somewhat stunned silence. Then Edward inquired with polite interest:

"How old are you, then?"

"Edward, that will do!" Aunt Katherine was divided between the pleasurable suspicion that Leigh really meant what he said, and chagrin that her son should have spoilt a touching moment.

"My goodness!" muttered Edward. "This is an extraord'nary family! All this fuss about getting me here, and then when I ask an intelligent question someone says 'That will do' again."

"Too bad, old man." Leigh smiled at him with unexpected sympathy. "You may take it that I am a good fifteen years older than your cousin." And he turned back to Aunt Katherine, leaving Edward rather obviously in the throes of mental arithmetic.

"Well, of course, I'm *simply delighted* to hear you say this." Aunt Katherine beamed upon him. "And I must say that no one could make a nicer wife than Nicola." She glanced round, noted her own four darlings, and added: "In the ordinary way."

"I knew you would feel like that," Leigh answered her smoothly, and Aunt Katherine really began to think she did.

"Do we all give you a sort of ceremonious kiss of welcome to the family circle?" inquired Diana obligingly.

"I won't insist upon such a charming attention," Leigh replied, with a hint of firmness. "Nicola is capable of doing that for you all." And, still with that air of self-possession, he kissed Nicola—this time on her mouth. And Nicola made the astonishing discovery that she really enjoyed kissing him back again.

Somehow she had never thought of Leigh bothering to make a social success of himself. Conforming to the conventional standard of pleasant society—yes. But that he should put himself out to be unusually amusing and charming had never entered into her expectations.

That evening, however, there was no doubt about it. Leigh was a success with the family—and he meant to be. Even Anne thawed, while Edward regarded him with respect, and withdrew with even more than usual reluctance when the tocsin of bedtime sounded.

Only once was there a jarring note, and that was when Diana said carelessly:

"I suppose Piers will be best man?"

"I hardly think so." Leigh's tone was cool, polite and final.

133

"Not?—but isn't he the obvious person?" Diana, with characteristic lack of tact, pursued the subject.

"Perhaps," Leigh agreed casually. "But I doubt if he'll be back in time."

"Back?" Diana looked surprised. Indeed they all did, and Nicola felt nervous and uncomfortable. "What's happened to him?"

"He was called away on a business trip very suddenly this—afternoon."

"But good gracious, he can't be away a very long time if it's at such short notice," Diana protested.

"It will be a matter of several weeks." Leigh was still perfectly cool. "And Nicola and I don't want a long engagement. So, as there's a likelihood of his *not* being back, the obvious thing is for us to choose someone else."

When he was going, Nicola came with him into the hall.

"Leigh, I'm going to walk down a little way with you."

He smiled and, without a word, took her coat from its peg and held it for her.

"Oh, I don't need that!"

"Yes, you do. It's chilly now."

She submitted, a trifle amusedly.

"How did you know which was mine?"

"Do I look short-sighted?"

"No. But—oh, I never imagined your noticing anything I wore. Besides, I don't think you've seen me wear this often. I certainly haven't come over to Thorpe Compton in it, because it's my 'country walk' coat."

"I've seen you wear it," was all he said, but he didn't offer to specify the occasion.

134

As she walked down the short drive with him, a large, warm golden moon was rising behind the trees and the first midsummer stars were pricking the sky.

It was a romantic night. The kind of night when some men—Piers, for instance—would have made love to one as a matter of course. Leigh, relieved now of the necessity of seeming devoted, presumably thought nothing else was required of him, for he actually said, in his most employer-like tone:

"I suppose I can expect you to-morrow as usual?"

"Why, of—of course."

"Good, There's rather a lot I want to get through."

"Very well. I'll be in good time." She nearly called him "Mr. Mason" once more at that moment, and she wondered how she could bring the conversation back to what had happened that evening.

Apparently he thought there was no reason to, in any case, because almost immediately afterwards he stopped and said:

"Don't come any farther, Nicola. I don't like the idea of your walking back alone. This is quite far enough."

"Very well."

She held out her hand. Then, as his fingers closed over hers, she reached up suddenly and kissed him of her own accord.

"Thank you, Leigh—awfully."

He laughed and said: "What's this for? Good practice?" But he took her face between his hands and kissed her before he sent her back with an almost peremptory "Now go along home."

When Nicola returned, the other were lounging about in comfortable family conclave.

"You've picked a winner, Nic," Diana remarked without preamble.

"He certainly seems intelligent," Anne admitted, while Caroline said once more:

"You're extremely lucky, Nicola," as though she could hardly understand how such an undistinguished person as Nicola *could* be so lucky.

"Why didn't he want Piers for best man?" Bridget wanted to know.

"I don't know that it was a case of not wanting," Nicola said hastily. "If he won't be back in time, that settles it."

"Perhaps so. Odd, though, that he seemed so determined not to have him."

"I think," Diana said slowly, "that the really odd thing was his absolute certainty that Piers wouldn't be back in time. Just as though he'd murdered him, and popped him under the middle dahlia bed in the garden."

"Diana! You do say the most unfortunate and *tasteless* things!" exclaimed poor Aunt Katherine.

They all laughed—even Nicola. But afterwards she thought, with a curiosity that was far from pleasant:

"Well, why *was* Leigh so sure, in any case? Diana was right—it *was* odd."

CHAPTER X

"Well, my dear, it looks as though your reputation is saved. Miss Pottington met me in the village to-day and asked me how many guests there would be, and if the service would be fully choral."

Diana tossed off her hat and smiled across good-temperedly at Nicola, who was sucking the top of her fountain-pen and struggling with the problem of a grateful letter of thanks for a wedding present she particularly detested.

Nicola nodded.

"She told Aunt Katherine she thought I would make 'a nice bride', so I knew then that my one wild oat was beginning to take on a cultivated air in the eyes of the village."

Diana subsided into a chair in an attitude that would have been ungraceful in anyone else but which, in her, only served to show off her enchanting figure.

"Funny that if you plonk 'Mrs.' in front of your name, all is forgiven and forgotten, so far as the Miss Pottingtons of this world are concerned," she said reflectively. "I wonder just how much she *would* swallow in that cause."

"You weren't thinking of testing that, were you?" Nicola inquired ironically. "I think I've provided enough family scandal for one year."

"Too true," Diana admitted. "But how gracefully Leigh has gilded it." Then, after another reflective pause: "I suppose you wouldn't tell me—just for private home consumption, whether you did really kick over the traces a bit?"

"Certainly not!" Nicola was indignant.

"Do you mean—certainly you wouldn't tell me or—certainly you didn't kick over the traces?" inquired Diana unperturbed.

"Di, you are ridiculous! I mean, certainly I didn't and wouldn't do such a thing—and anyway, I shouldn't tell you if I did."

"So we're just where we started," Diana remarked. Nicola laughed crossly.

"You don't really think I'm that sort of girl, do you?"

"I haven't the slightest idea," Diana replied equably. "I think in some ways you're rather a dark horse, and I can imagine that if you were absolutely mad about Leigh——"

"But I'm not absolutely mad about Leigh!" interrupted Nicola hastily.

"No," Diane said. "No, I've noticed that."

Nicola looked faintly uncomfortable.

"I'm very fond of him," she explained earnestly.

"That must be lovely," Diana yawned.

Nicola didn't pursue the subject. Instead she said:

"Can you think of a graceful ending to a letter of thanks, when you don't really like the thing you're acknowledging?"

"No," Diana said, "I can't. I seldom think—and almost never in terms of gratitude.'

"Di!" Nicola laughed protestingly. "And yet—do you know—I like you best of the family."

"I'm sure you do. I'm the most likeable," Diana agreed. "I'm good-tempered, completely undemanding and practically never shocked. In addition, I always give people the pleasurable feeling that they're cleverer than I am, without making them uncomfortable by emphasizing the fact that I'm prettier than they are. I often think how comfortable I must be to live with."

And Diana complacently retired to the silent contemplation of her finger-nails, which she presently began to manicure with absorbed attention.

Nicola, for her part, finished the letter, and then turned her attention to an imposing writing-pad at her elbow on which appeared, in Aunt Katherine's strong, legible handwriting the two words, "Nicola's Wedding", and then a list of jobs still to be attended to.

It was more than a month now since that strange afternoon when Nicola had run back across the fields to tell Leigh Mason she would marry him, and in very much less than another month she would be putting that into practice.

Even now she found it difficult to realize that she had actually committed herself to marrying anyone—perhaps least of all Leigh Mason, for there were still often times when he treated her exactly like a secretary and not in the least like a fiancée.

"I suppose," reflected Nicola, not without humour, "those are the times when it just slips his memory that he *is* going to marry me."

He always treated her with devoted attention in front of people, and he certainly had presented her with an engagement ring which made the Round family gasp appreciatively. But sometimes, when they were working alone in his study at Thorpe Compton, he would comment on her work or give his instructions as though he never saw her as anything but an efficient secretary who, so far, had given him no reason to sack her.

During all this time Nicola had neither seen nor heard anything of Piers, but if she thought his behaviour extremely cavalier there was no one with whom she could discuss it. None of the family even knew the facts of the case, except Aunt Katherine—and she had long ago written him off as an irresponsible young man who had ceased to have anything to do with her family. It was doubtful if she often, if ever, recalled his existence, once he had been voted unsuitable in the only possible role of best man.

Leigh, of course, in the ordinary way, would have been the person with whom to discuss him. But Leigh on the subject of Piers was always disconcerting. If he thought the silence both rude and inexplicable he said nothing about it. And if he thought Piers had any adequate reason for it, at least he never tried to vindicate him. In fact, since he refused to open the subject himself, Nicola was forced to ignore it too.

"It's rather stupid," she had sometimes thought impatiently, "that I can't even bring myself to ask Leigh if he's told Piers about our wedding." But somehow, she told herself from day to day that surely Piers would be back soon, and then the problem would solve itself.

Now, as she absently read down Aunt Katherine's list of "things still to be done", she thought with overwhelming urgency:

"But much more important than these is the question of explaining to Piers. It's too absurd that he's simply been shelved as though he had ceased to exist.

I shall speak to Leigh to-morrow."

Determination had waned somewhat by the time she faced Leigh across the study next morning, but she forced herself to keep to her intention.

"Leigh"—she pretended to be busy opening a letter, but became aware almost immediately that he knew her casualness was assumed—"tell me, have you heard anything from Piers?"

"No. Did you think I should have?"

"Well, I—I supposed you'd written to him about —things."

"Telling him we were getting married, you mean?"

"Of course."

"I wasn't able to." He was casual too—and suddenly she realized, with astounding certainty, that *his* casualness was assumed.

Somehow there was something most incongruous about Leigh having to assume casualness, instead of having it clothe him as naturally as his own well-cut suit.

"Why didn't—I mean, why couldn't you tell him?"

"Because he left no address, my dear. Piers went on an extended tour of inspection in connection with his work. I know roughly the ground he's covering, but have no idea when he'll be at any special place. Since he didn't supply me with any address, I presume he had no special wish to hear from me."

"But isn't it—rather self-conscious to carry things so far as that? Surely you could write to his head office or something like that?"

"I suppose I could if I wanted to, but I can't imagine that Piers would be so passionately interested in what I did with myself."

Nicola was silent. The difficulty was, of course, that Piers would be interested from *her* point of view, not Leigh's.

Perhaps that point struck him because, after a moment, he looked across at her rather dryly and said:

"If you feel Piers ought to know, why not write to him yourself? I can give you his office address and the letter will be forwarded, no doubt."

"I think it would come better from you." Nicola made that curt because she felt Leigh was behaving with less than his usual consideration.

"Believe me," Leigh retorted coldly, "Piers would find it more than strange to receive a letter from me on any subject." And then, apparently considering the matter entirely closed, he returned to the paper he had been reading.

For some reason she could not define, Nicola found her temper rising, out of all proportion to the conversation.

"Will you give me the address, then, please?" She spoke at least as coldly as he.

If he sensed her anger, he ignored it, merely scribbling the address on a piece of paper and passing it over to her without any comment.

"Thank you." For a moment or two she twisted the paper in her hands, toying with the idea of telling him just how ridiculous she thought his attitude was. Then she recalled that they were something like ten days from their wedding day, and to start quarrelling about Piers, considering the circumstances, would be more than foolish.

So she swallowed her anger somehow and, so far

as she was aware, Leigh remained ignorant of the fact that he had irritated her profoundly.

It was not until she was in her own bedroom that night that she sat down to write to Piers. Not that she intended to write a specially private and intimate letter. But in the Round household it was always rather difficult, somehow, to do anything a little delicate without exciting comment and query. As a family, they had a remarkable sense of detecting what one preferred to keep to oneself. Aunt Katherine, in particular, was, of course, a brilliant home detective.

When she sat down to the task, Nicola imagined it would be fairly easy for, after all, she and Piers had always been frank with each other. But, when it came to explaining just *why* they were doing this thing, she realized that the task was anything but simple.

Perhaps, reflected Nicola, it was the same discovery which had influenced Leigh in his decision to write nothing.

To state, in cold blood, the real facts seemed, somehow, a sort of betrayal of the effort she and Leigh were making to give the whole thing an air of decency. It would be, in fact, an offence against whatever loyalty she owed Leigh for extricating her from the situation.

And yet to expect Piers—who, with all his careless good nature, was a cynic at heart—to accept the story prepared for the artless Miss Pottington's consumption——! No, that really would be futile.

"I'll have to compromise," thought Nicola. And, after much thought and a considerable waste of paper, she wrote:

*Dear Piers,—I'm sending this to your London of-
fice, in the hope that it will be forwarded to you
before long. I would have written earlier but for the
fact that I expected you home before now, but I don't
feel it is reasonable to delay sending you the news
any longer. Leigh and I are being married on the
fifteenth.*

*I'm sure it will be a surprise for you, and I hardly
know how to explain what led up to it. Of course, the
gossip and scandal in the village was the first thing
that put the idea into our minds but, once it was
there, I suppose we began to regard each other in a
rather different light. Anyway, whether we intended
it or not, we were inevitably coupled together and—
well, the truth is, Piers, that we found we liked it!*

*I wish you could have been home in time for the
wedding, but Leigh doesn't seem to think it's at all
likely. If you do manage it, however, you know how
delighted I shall be.—Yours, Nicola.*

She had nearly put: "You know how delighted *we*
shall be", but, remembering just how Piers and Leigh
regarded each other, she decided to sacrifice convention
to truth.

As an afterthought, she added a P.S.

*At any rate, this arrangement relieves you of any
possible anxiety about unwelcome disclosures,
doesn't it?*

Nicola didn't much care for the letter, when she
read it over. It seemed stiff and unnatural, particularly
when she thought on what easy terms she and Piers
had always been. But no amount of thought and care

would make the telling of such news an easy matter—in the circumstances. And so she decided to content herself with what was written, sealed the envelope, and went to bed, to dream that, by a series of mistakes, she found herself married to Piers instead of Leigh.

The letter was posted next morning and, for a day or two, Nicola somehow expected a reply by return of post. There was no reason why there should be, of course, for, whatever arrangement he had made for forwarding letters, the delay might still be one of several days.

After a little while, Nicola accepted that fact, and the nearness of her wedding made everything else—even the Piers situation—seem unimportant by contrast.

In spite of all Aunt Katherine's efforts, Nicola and Leigh had succeeded in keeping the wedding preparations to moderate proportions. It seemed they might even be allowed to have a fairly quiet and inconspicuous wedding—except that, naturally, most of the village intended to turn up at the church.

On the afternoon before her wedding, Nicola found —rather to her amusement—that she was even more than usually busy. Leigh had arranged that they should have at any rate a week's honeymoon, if only to satisfy Aunt Katherine and, in consequence, there was a good deal that had to be cleared up in his work beforehand.

"I'm sorry, Nicola. I'm afraid I'm driving you rather hard this afternoon," he said once.

"That's all right." Nicola smiled at him. "When a man gets married, I suppose his secretary is bound to have a busy time of it in the last-minute rush."

"A very broad-minded view to take," Leigh said, and smiled too.

"Oh well, I don't really mind," Nicola explained. "To tell the truth, I'd much rather be here working than at home in the midst of wedding consultations with Aunt Katherine. She knows exactly what I ought to want, whereas I don't. It's so much simpler to let her work it out her own way, without opposition."

"Oh, quite," agreed Leigh a trifle dryly, and Nicola wondered, in some surprise, if he minded her speaking of her wedding like that. After all, no one could be more formal than he, or more official. She ought to be allowed a little flippancy about her wedding in return!

Not until the church clock was striking six did he exclaim:

"I can't keep you here any longer, Nicola. The rest will have to wait until we come home from—our honeymoon. Go along now, child. I don't know what on earth your aunt will think as it is."

Nicola thoughtfully clipped papers together, tidied her desk and covered her typewriter. And all the while she was overwhelmingly aware, for the first time, that a definite chapter of her life was closing.

She would be coming back to this work, of course. In no more than a week she would be taking up things just where she had left them. But it would not be the same. She would no longer be Nicola Round, engaged as Leigh Mason's secretary. She would be Nicola Mason who—because of their mutual interest in his work—chose to go on helping her husband.

She slipped on her coat and began to pull on her gloves, making rather a long business of it. He was not watching her, but she knew he was very much aware of her. And when she was finally ready, he seemed to know it, to the second, because he stood up, before she could say anything, and came round to where she was standing.

"Good-bye, my dear. I shan't be seeing you again until I see you in church tomorow, so——"

"Yes?" Nicola said, as he stopped, in unusual hesitation.

"Well, Nicola"—he thrust his hands into his pockets and smiled with less than his usual assurance—"I don't know what else I ought to say to you at this moment. I only want you to know that—I'll look after you to the best of my ability, and really try to make you happy. We aren't going to help ourselves or each other by talking any more about the peculiar circumstances. Let's just try to accept those and make what we can of the rest."

"Thank you, Leigh." She was unexpectedly touched by this speech. Partly because she had practically never seen him look nervous before, and partly because she felt sure he had thought it out very carefully in order to reassure her. "I don't see why we shouldn't make a success of it."

And then, because she could think of nothing else to say, but felt that it would be abrupt to leave things just like that, she reached up and kissed him.

Putting his arm round her, he returned the kiss, with as much an air of devotion as if the whole Round family were watching. And then Nicola went home—her secretarial career as Miss Round entirely at an end.

She went through the garden, because she intended

to walk home across the fields and, late though she was, she lingered for a moment or two, to savour the beauties of what would soon be her own garden. The idea was pleasurable, and yet in a curious way, frightening. She had been nobody for so long that it was hard to realize that, as Leigh Mason's wife, she would be "somebody". Somebody with an exceptionally beautiful house and garden of her own. Somebody with a celebrated husband, come to that!

She was smiling thoughtfully as she came through the garden gateway into the fields. And, as she did so, her arm was eagerly seized by someone, and Piers's voice exclaimed:

"Nicola! I thought you were never coming!"

"Piers!" Astonishment was almost more than pleasure at that moment. "But when did you arrive? And what are you doing here, instead of coming into the house?"

"I was waiting for you. I don't want to go into the house. Do you suppose I intend to talk to you in front of Leigh? I want to talk to you alone."

"But, Piers——" she was suddenly apprehensive, "there's nothing we have to say which Leigh couldn't hear."

"My dear, don't be ridiculous." In his eagerness and anxiety, Piers didn't stop to pick his words. Still holding her arm, he fell into step beside her, determinedly leading her away from Thorpe Compton, as though he almost thought she might insist on going back there and making Leigh a witness of whatever they did and said.

"I got your letter only this morning, when I called in at my office in town. They had instructions not to

148

send on anything during the last ten days as I didn't know where I would be. I came at once." He spoke in quick, jerky phrases, and then burst out: "What is this absurd, iniquitous idea? You and Leigh! It's unthinkable. I won't have it!"

"Piers——" She withdrew her arm very firmly, whether he liked it or not. "It's you who are being absurd. There's no question of *you're* 'having' it. The arrangement has nothing to do with you—it's our own private affair."

"Nic, don't talk like that!—as though I'm a stranger, with no right to care about what you do. You know quite well what you mean to me. You must have known. It was in everything I said and did."

With a strange little chill of dismay, Nicola stopped short in her walk.

"You musn't talk like this. There was never anything said between us that could—that could—well, I mean, I hadn't any reason to think you had a personal interest in whatever I did. Apart from the interest of a friend, of course."

"A friend! My dear girl, we were not just friends. You know we were much more."

"I'm sorry." Nicola's tone was firm, though she was trembling slightly. "I don't say it would have altered things even if I had known you regarded me as more than a friend. But there was nothing, Piers, that *could* give me that idea—beyond the fact that we were friendly and, I suppose, we flirted sometimes."

"It was much more than that." His voice was low and full of feeling. "I thought you understood."

"What was I to understand?" She looked at him with very direct gaze suddenly. "Are you trying to say that once you'd divorced your wife, you hoped to marry me?"

Even then, Nicola had the curious impression that Piers would not have put the idea into actual words. But he nodded, in answer to her question, his eyes dark with an expression of unhappy appeal.

"I'm sorry." She put her hand on his arm. "Indeed, I'm sorry, Piers dear, but——"

"Did you never suspect how I felt?"

"Well, at first, I thought—I wondered a little if that was what was going to happen. But afterwards—" —she shook her head—"afterwards, quite frankly, Piers, I thought you weren't at all serious."

"But if you'd known, Nic!" He caught her hand in his and held it painfully tight. "If you'd known how I felt, you would never have started this ridiculous business with Leigh, would you?"

"How do I know what I would have done?" She tried, unsuccessfully, to draw her hand away. "I *didn't* know how you felt, and it isn't any good going over that now. The point is that I'm engaged to Leigh —that I'm going to marry him to-morrow."

"To-morrow!"

"Why, yes. I told you in the letter. The fifteenth."

"Good lord!" He passed his hand over his forehead. "I hadn't realized it was such a near thing. Thank God I came at once."

"There's nothing for you to do, Piers, even though you have come at once," she pointed out rather firmly. "Except, of course, that I'm glad to have you there at the wedding."

"I don't intend that there shall be a wedding!" Piers said violently. "The whole idea is monstrous."

150

"Please!" In something very like anger, Nicola turned on him. "You've no right whatever to speak like that. Leigh and I have our own reasons for doing what we *are* doing, and they have nothing to do with you. I'm sorry—I'm very sorry—if you're hurt about it. But I don't think you have any reason to reproach me. You never said clearly that you—that you loved me. I know the fact that you were married probably helped to silence you. But you should have been more frank with me, if you wanted me to understand. You didn't behave much like a man who wanted to marry me over that miserable business at the inn."

He started and looked at her with a quick glance of unhappy protest. Then, as though admitting the justice of what she said, he nodded grimly.

"You've every right to reproach me, Nic. I hadn't realized——"

"I'm not reproaching you!" She was extremly distressed. "I'm not reproaching you at all. I'm only explaining why it was that I thought as I did. Please, Piers, don't let's talk of reproach and blame. You had your reasons for acting as you did. I have mine for acting as I am acting now. What's the good of asking ourselves what we would have done if things had been quite different? It only makes one miserable and——"

"You mean to say you're perfectly willing to let Leigh get away with it?"

"*Leigh?* What has Leigh to do with this? It's no fault of his if you and I didn't understand each other. He's behaved perfectly throughout, whatever mistakes and foolishness we have indulged in."

"Nic, dear, you can't be so ingenuous. Why do you

suppose Leigh chose his time so carefully?—because I was out of the way, of course. When he did make this suggestion of marrying you, by the way?—not long after I had gone, I'll be bound."

Nicola paled slightly, and refused to answer that until Piers pressed her.

"It was the same day," she admitted reluctantly because she knew Piers would read some significance into that.

"There! What did I say?" He was angrily triumphant. "My God, he didn't waste much time! He knew I'd have opposed the idea tooth and nail, quite apart from my own feelings, so he reckoned to get the whole business settled before I came back."

"You're imagining things, Piers."

"I'm not. Why do you suppose he never wrote to me about it? Do you think it's natural for people who know each other as well as I and Leigh just to overlook a little detail like the marriage of one of them?"

"He—he said you left no address."

"But he could have got me at the office."

"Frankly, he didn't think you'd be particularly interested in his affairs, Piers. You've never shown any liking for him, and——"

"Not interested? He knew I'd be a damn sight too interested in this. Surely, Nic, you can see how odd it is that only an hour or two after I've gone off he proposes to you, tries to rush the wedding through in a matter of weeks, and refuses even to write, letting me know what's happened?"

"But there's an explanation for all that!"

Because of her instinctive uneasiness, Nicola was emphatic in her protest.

"What explanation?"

"Well, it just happened that that afternoon the gossiping came to a head, and then we discussed this idea and—and liked it a good deal more than you seem willing to believe. And if we were going to do it at all, obviously we had to do it quickly. And as for the not writing—well, I've *told* you the reason for that."

"Things like that just don't *happen*," Piers protested scornfully.

"But it's ridiculous, Piers! From any point of argument it's ridiculous. Why should Leigh want to do this? Even if he doesn't like you—even if he were petty enough to want to do something that would make you miserable—surely you don't suppose he would go to the lengths of marrying someone just to spite you?"

"Just to—what?"

Piers stopped dead in his tracks and stared at her.

"Well—" she was faintly disconcerted by his expression—"well, isn't that what you're trying to imply?'

"My dear girl," Piers said slowly, "can it possibly have escaped your notice that, in his odd way, Leigh is crazily in love with you?"

CHAPTER XI

Nicola stared at Piers for a moment in silent astonishment. Then she said slowly:

"Leigh!—in love with me? Oh, no, Piers, you've got that wrong. That is—if you really mean—mean—" she floundered helplessly, because she hardly knew how to express her belief in Leigh's kindly indifference to her and at the same time continue to give the impression of a decent amount of feeling between two people who were about to marry. "Leigh is very fond of me," she began at last, but Piers brushed that aside impatiently.

"Leigh's infatuated with you in his self-controlled and—and bloodless way. He never meant me to get you. That was why he was always interfering whenever you and I got on too well for his liking. Of course, this damned business at the inn gave him a chance to be coupled with you, and when he found I was going away for several weeks, he simply leapt at the chance of going behind my back and getting things fixed before I could return. I bet he practically forbade you to write to me, didn't he?"

"Certainly not," retorted Nicola with spirit. "We are not on the 'forbidding' footing."

"Well, then he discouraged the idea. Isn't that right?" She was silent, and he exclaimed in angry triumph: "I knew it! Surely you can see for yourself how he stage-managed things, Nic?"

She bit her lip. There was something in what he

said, of course. Only his explanation was ridiculous. There couldn't be anything in that. She didn't want to believe there was anything in it because—Oh, because it would mean such extraordinary and disturbing complications if Leigh really *were* in love with her.

As though instinctively avoiding the subject, her mind turned to another aspect of the question, and she said suddenly:

"There is one other thing that needs some explaining, Piers. If you were suspicious of all this and—and felt so strongly about me, why did *you* never write to *me* all those weeks? You knew my address. We had parted excellent friends. And yet you never even bothered to write an explanation of why you'd gone away, or—or the smallest note of greeting."

He looked taken aback for a moment, then he flushed.

"Oh—that! Don't imagine I didn't want to write. Only—" he hesitated, and then went on doggedly— "I knew you were feeling pretty wild with me because you thought I'd done the wrong thing over that business at the inn. I thought if you didn't hear for a bit you might—well, begin to think of me a little more kindly."

"Teaching me a lesson, in fact?"

"No, Nic, it wasn't that. I swear to you I didn't think of it in those terms."

"Very well." She smiled faintly at his boyish earnestness. "It doesn't matter now. I only wondered——"

"Yes, of course. And it *does* matter. If I hadn't been such a fool, I should have heard long ago about this ridiculous marriage idea, and come home and scotched it."

"But are you so sure that you had only to come

155

home in order to do that?" Nicola's tone was a trifle cool.

"Nic, for God's sake, let's be frank! You're not *pining* to marry Leigh, are you?"

She was angry suddenly at that. She didn't want to have to analyse her feelings and her reasons all over again. She had fought out this issue to herself, and the conclusion had been reached. It was useless for Piers to come now and try to upset everything, with the vague protestation that he himself hoped to marry her at some future date when he could get rid of his present wife.

"I'm not going to discuss it any more, Piers." Her tone was firm. "I've made my decision, and so has Leigh. We—we believe we can make each other happy, and I'm not going to spoil things by regrets over something that might—or might not, have happened, if circumstances had been different. Please, please let us leave it at that."

"I don't think you're facing even now the unpleasantness of discovering that Leigh—to whom you're completely indifferent—will, quite literally, be your loving husband this time tomorrow," Piers exclaimed angrily.

Nicola lost a little colour.

"You're letting your imagination run away with you," she said coldly. "But, in any case, it's my own business. I must go now, Piers. I'm frightfully late already. Aunt Katherine will wonder what on earth I'm doing." She held out her hand to him. "Shall I—shall I see you tomorrow?"

"When Leigh marries you?" He gave an angry laugh. "No, Nicola, you must excuse me. I mayn't

156

be squeamish, but I'm not coming to *that* wedding."
And with the slightest touch of his hand on hers, he
turned away and left her.

Even then she wanted to run after him and demand
angrily—and a little fearfully—what he had meant by
that last remark. What was there about her marriage
to Leigh that should make anyone feel "squeamish"?
He wanted to imply, of course, that she would have
someone on her hands who was fond to a most unwelcome degree. It was ridiculous! And yet——

She actually turned back towards Thorpe Compton,
more than half determined to go and face Leigh with
the charge, and receive his half sarcastic but reassuring
denial.

But she could not. She told herself it was because it
was much too late and she should be home already—
that she could hardly make a fool of herself like that
in front of Leigh—that it would be embarrassing for
them both to discuss such an absurd suggestion.

But, as she turned slowly back in the direction of
home, she knew at the bottom of her heart why she
would not go back and face Leigh. She was afraid.
For what could she do if he admitted, by the thou-
sandth chance, that Piers was right? It was too late to
alter anything now. And yet, if he did feel like that——

Nicola broke into a run as she crossed the last field,
and she didn't stop running until the ascent to Aunt
Katherine's house left her too breathless to run any
more.

Nicola used to think afterwards that she had a comparatively minor role at her own wedding. To have
supposed that she could possibly be the star performer

—when not only Aunt Katherine, but also Aunt Katherine's four daughters, were present—would have been nothing less than indulging in wishful thinking. And, when the time came, Nicola rather thought that even she herself was more impressed by Aunt Katherine's air of magnificent bounty as she "gave away" her niece than by anything else about the ceremony.

Nearly all Longheedon, of course, turned out to see Nicola well and truly married, partly because a free show was never to be despised, but mostly because there had been what were now referred to as "stories" about the central figures.

Nicola sensed—or fancied she sensed—even more than the usual rustle of interest as she and Aunt Katherine entered the church. And while Aunt Katherine dispensed smiles and gracious little bows on every hand, garnering every glance of interest and enjoying it to the full—the bride was secretly thinking:

"Well, I hope this is the last time they will take such a passionate interest in me. Perhaps *now* they will allow my one little indiscretion to die a natural death!"

Strange to reflect, that that same "little indiscretion" really had nothing to do with the tall, dark man who was waiting for her now at the end of the long aisle. He was simply the man who had covered her tracks for her—saved her face—whatever you liked to call it.

In that moment, Nicola thought of him as the man who had rescued her. Rescued her from the curiosity and censure of the people who now were watching her from what seemed like every angle of the church.

There was something slightly panic-stricken in the glance with which she met Leigh's grave smile and, as though he read a great deal more than was written in her pale, tense young face, he calmly put out his hand and drew her gently towards him, with a suggestion of warmth and affection which, most surprisingly, made her want to cry.

Everyone in the church must have seen him, slight though the movement was. And it was as though he told everyone there, in his perfectly cool and unmistakable fashion, that he was not marrying this girl because their gossip had forced him to, but because he loved her and wanted to look after her.

"It was only done for effect, of course," Nicola was telling herself all through the "Dearly Beloved—" "He didn't mean it really. But, oh, how sweet of him! How absolutely dear and—*clever*!"

It had been agreed with Aunt Katherine (in theory) that the wedding breakfast afterwards should be "little more than a family party". But in the end the company swelled to considerably larger proportions than that description warranted, and certainly most of them would have been hard put to it to establish any connection whatever with the family.

To Nicola it seemed a somewhat overwhelming gathering, and she found herself thinking—"I shall be thankful to be alone with Leigh. At least—I shall be thankful not to have so many people round me."

Everyone was in a terrific flutter of congratulation, and none more so than the ladies who had most eagerly condemned her before this happy and respectable conclusion to her story.

Even Miss Pottington—drifting up with a sandwich in one hand and "just a tiny, tiny glass of port" in the other—was full of congratulations.

"Dear Nicola, you looked *charming*. And he is *most*

distinguished-looking. A delightful wedding altogether. Your dear aunt must be a happy woman to-day."

Nicola said, with all sincerity, that she hoped her aunt was a happy woman.

"Everyone wishes you so well, dear," went on Miss Pottington, becoming even more expansive as she neared the bottom of her tiny, tiny glass. "And, as one might say, bygones are indeed bygones."

Nicola wondered if she were supposed to show some sort of gratitude for this charitable reflection. She felt both annoyed and embarrassed, and would willingly have turned away to one of her other guests, but Miss Pottington intended to say all she had come to say.

"Even Angela sent you her best wishes—her *respectful* wishes, I might say."

"Angela?" Nicola sought in vain for any memory of an Angela among her acquaintances.

"Yes. My new daily help, you know."

Miss Pottington had a constant succession of daily helps who, as new brooms, invariably swept clean, but as invariably departed about two months later with every bristle on end.

"Oh, that was very kind of her," murmured Nicola politely. "But she hasn't ever seen me, has she?"

"Well, dear Nicola, as a matter of fact, she *has*." Miss Pottington gave a meaning smile. "I suppose that is why she took so much interest. She was working at —well, shall I just say a certain inn. And she was very, very glad to hear that all had ended happily."

At this impertinence—quite astonishing even for Miss Pottington—Nicola felt the angry colour flood into her face. Then it ebbed away again, as the full implication of the announcement began to dawn upon her.

Of course! She meant that wretched girl at the inn, who—through stupidity or sheer misfortune—had set in motion all the unfortunate events of the last few weeks. The girl who had started off the scandal with her ill-chosen "Mr. Mason's still in the bedroom, miss."

Nicola felt so vexed and humiliated and, somehow, scared that she hardly knew what to say in the first moment. Then, becoming aware that Miss Pottington's bright, inquisitive eyes were observing her with curiosity and a touch of malice, she pulled herself together and said coldly:

"Something of a coincidence, surely, that she should happen to come and work for you, Miss Pottington?"

"Oh, no—" Miss Pottington was full of the most natural explanations. "No, dear Nicola, not at all. She was very obliging and bright over some service I required of her when we were there that—that rather unfortunate morning."

("Submitted to being pumped, I suppose," reflected Nicola savagely. "I can't imagine any other way in which she would be bright.")

"I talked with her just a little, you know," pursued Miss Pottington cheerfully, "and found that she was not at all happy in her work—no doubt a very *mixed clientele* at such a place—and I offered her a job with me."

"I see."

Nicola made that so dry that, for once, perhaps even Miss Pottington realized that her hearer had "seen" rather more than she had intended. At any rate, she smiled vaguely and moved away again, murmuring something entirely mendacious about not wanting to take up *too* much of the bride's time.

There was no time to examine this exasperating new development at leisure because, even as Nicola turned away, biting her lip with vexation, Diana came up to her and said:

"It's about time you went up to change, you know. I'll come too and pretend to help you, since that's the bridesmaid's conventional role. Though I don't expect marriage has robbed you of your ability to put on your own clothes."

"Thanks. Yes, do come too. I want to talk to you."

Diana looked amused and faintly mystified at that, but she came up to Nicola's bedroom where, laid out on the bed was the green travelling dress and the little squirrel cape which Aunt Katherine's characteristic generosity had supplied.

"That's sweet." Diana ran her hand critically over the dark, silky fur. "And it's just right with that rather cheekily-engenuous little hat."

"Yes." Nicola smiled, but absently. "Aunt Katherine was awfully generous about my outfit."

There was silence for a moment or two, while Nicola slipped out of her wedding dress, and Diana lounged gracefully in a chair by the window, without any attempt to carry out her conventional duties.

"What was it you wanted to talk about?" she inquired indolently at last.

"I wanted to let off steam to someone," Nicola retorted viciously as she jerked the green dress over her head. "I could *kill* Miss Pottington."

"You'd earn the everlasting gratitude of quite a number of people, if you did," Diana assured her without heat. "What's she been doing now?' '

"Di, would you believe it? She's hunted out the

chambermaid from that—that inn, and now the wretched girl is installed as Miss P's latest daily help."

Diana opened her large blue eyes very wide. Then she said:

"I shouldn't worry. She'll have got rid of her almost before you're home from your honeymoon."

"Oh, no, she won't. She'll hang on to this one. She may last two or three months."

"I suppose," Diana agreed reflectively, "that an ex-barmaid *could* supply Miss Pottington with some handsome tit-bits of gossip."

"Oh, she wasn't a barmaid, Di. I suppose you'd call her a chambermaid."

"Better and better from Miss P's point of view," Diana remarked cheerfully. "But don't bother about it, Nic. *You're* respectably married now, and there isn't anything the little darling can add to your story. At least—I suppose not?" That was half a question, and Nicola turned away to the mirror without answering it.

Again there was a short silence, while Di studied her cousin's back. Then she said:

"Don't spoil your honeymoon worrying over this. What you and Leigh did or didn't do hardly matters in Miss Pottington's eyes now. And she's sure to have a blow-up with this girl eventually. You know she always does. Then everything the poor little wretch has said will be discredited, whether it's true or untrue. You may yet come into your own again as an unspotted lily."

"I wonder if you're right." Nicola gave a worried little shrug.

"I quite often am," Diana claimed modestly. "And

163

anyway, I never think that worrying helps much, do you? It only makes one nervous if a crisis *does* come."

Nicola laughed.

"You're very comforting, Di. I sometimes wonder if you aren't the cleverest of us all in some ways."

"So do I," Diana agreed. "But we won't tell Anne —Ready now? Really, Nic, you're almost pretty in that."

"Thanks. Do I need a little more colour?"

Her cousin studied her critically.

"No. I like that sort of honey-gold tan you have, without any pinkish additions. It's much more unusual. That green's brought up the colour of your eyes well. I wonder what colour one would call your eyes," she added reflectively.

"Leigh says they're real hazel."

"Oh—he's got as far as discussing the colour of your eyes, has he?"

"He mentioned that the first time we met," Nicola assured her with sudden amusement. And then Aunt Katherine came tapping on the door, with her cheerfully determined:

"Girls, girls! don't waste too much time talking. It's time Nicola was down."

Nicola went over and opened the door to her.

"I'm almost ready, Aunt Katherine."

Her aunt came in immediately, and proceeded to walk round her, commenting and criticizing from every angle.

"Charming, dear, charming! You certainly do pay for dressing, child."

"Thank you, Aunt Katherine. And thank you for all the lovely things you've given me, and—and arranging

164

all the wedding so marvellously."

"Oh, my dear Nicola, that's nothing. Nothing at all." Aunt Katherine didn't mean that literally, of course. She, too, thought she had managed everything marvellously. "All I want is to see you happy. And I think you will be with Leigh."

"So do I," Nicola assured her gravely. She thought for a moment of telling her aunt about the horrid and stupid new development at Miss Pottington's. Then she reflected that Diana was probably right, and the less attention that was paid to it, the less likely it was to cause unpleasantness.

So she went down stairs with her aunt and her cousin, to receive the last salvo of congratulations and good wishes, which ended in Edward solemnly throwing his football boots after the car, as Leigh and she drove away.

For a while they drove in silence. Then Leigh said, as casually as if he had only taken her out for a run in the car:

"Tired?"

She roused herself with a smile.

"No. Not at all. I'm rather glad all the fuss is over, though."

"And just a bit worried to find you're really married," he suggested with a smile.

"Well—yes. It's nice of you to understand, Leigh," she added impulsively.

"But it's not so difficult to understand. I think it's the most absolutely natural reaction. In fact—" the smile deepened—"I'm not sure that I don't feel a touch of it myself."

Nicola laughed then, and felt much more at ease. So

much at ease, that she suddenly found no difficulty in asking a question which had been troubling her a good deal.

"Leigh, did Piers leave again yesterday?—Or did he stay on and simply—refuse to come to the wedding?"

"Piers?" Her husband gave her a surprised glance. "Piers hasn't been home, surely! At least, I hadn't known it." He looked at her again, a trifle sternly, she thought.

She wished very much then that she had said nothing about Piers. Of course, what he had done was to go away again without even going into the house and seeing his cousin. Probably they had seen the last of him for a long while to come, and the subject would never have come up if she hadn't foolishly dragged it in herself. As it was, Leigh looked as though he considered he had asked a question and very definitely expected an answer from her.

"Well, I—didn't realize that he went away again without going into the house. He met—that is, I ran into him on the way home yesterday evening. He wanted to have a talk with me. I didn't understand that, having had it, he simply went away again."

"Would it be inquisitive," Leigh asked rather deliberately, " to inquire what it was that he wanted to discuss with you in private?"

"He was very—angry and distressed about our marriage, I'm afraid."

"How impertinent of him."

"Oh, no, Leigh, not really. He didn't mean it that way." She wished more than ever now that she had never embarked on this awkward topic but, having done so, she could hardly leave things here. "I suppose you knew he was—very much attached to me. He had some idea that I—that I——"

"Would wait until he had got rid of his present wife, and then see what he thought about taking another one."

"I think he imagined he had made it quite clear that *he* wanted to marry me when he was free," Nicola explained diffidently.

"Whereas, actually, he had never made himself clear at all, I suppose?" Leigh made that extremely dry.

"Not—very," Nicola admitted.

"And, in fact, never put anything into words until he found you had been snapped up by someone else. Whereupon you immediately became irresistible."

Nicola gave a vexed little laugh.

"Leigh, you're being very uncharitable."

"My dear, I'm looking the facts in the face. And, frankly, I don't find they look very agreeable."

"Please don't put the worst construction on them." Nicola was very much in earnest. "You make me very sorry now that I ever mentioned his coming."

"It didn't need the mention of that to make me see things as they are. You don't suppose I was unaware of Piers's pleasant, conscienceless philandering, do you? Or that I couldn't see that the last thing he wanted was to tie himself down, only he didn't intend anyone else to have you either. It's the old story, Nicola, of all the fun and none of the responsibility."

She bit her lip.

"I'm afraid you would never be very fair to Piers," she said distressedly.

"No, perhaps you're right." Unexpectedly he agreed

with her about that. "Particularly I should not be fair to him over this. One is never fair to the people of whom one is afraid."

"Afraid! Leigh, I can't imagine your being afraid of anyone! Why should you possibly be afraid of Piers?"

For a moment he seemed to realize what a strange thing he had said. Then he answered her, almost as though he were thinking aloud:

"He's so young, my dear. So plausible—so dangerous, almost without wishing to be. There's nothing I can set against his easy, convincing charm except a row of solid arguments. And what girl of twenty is interested in solid arguments?"

There was an extraordinary little silence. Then Nicola suddenly found there was something she had to know.

"Leigh, Piers said you had your reasons for—for engineering this marriage. That it wasn't just a question of silencing scandal. He said—" she glanced at her husband, but his profile told her nothing—"he said you were crazily in love with me. Leigh——" Her voice trailed away into silence.

He didn't look at her. He didn't even slacken the pace of the car. He simply said:

"Well, and suppose I am crazily in love with you—what about it?"

CHAPTER XII

Nicola had a ridiculous impulse to stammer: "Oh—nothing," like some silly little girl, and then change the subject with desperate haste. But of course, one could not leave a statement like that without a real answer.

"I—had no idea," she said at last, and was not sure that this was not as feeble as her first inspiration.

"There was no reason why you should," he assured her coolly.

"Oh, but Leigh—it's rather important."

"Important?" He gave a pleasant, slightly rueful laugh. "In the circumstances, I imagine it's little more than embarrassing."

"I'm not the slightest bit embarrassed," Nicola assured him with some energy. "Why on earth should I be?"

"Because to have a fond, elderly husband on your hands might be the height of discomfort," he assured her.

"Leigh, will you stop making these ridiculous, half-sarcastic remarks about yourself! You deliberately make yourself sound unattractive, whereas, in reality, you——"

"In reality?" he prompted, as she hesitated.

"I hadn't thought of it before," she confessed slowly. "But I suppose you're the most genuinely attractive man I've ever seen."

"Nicola dear, that's charming of you." He laughed, and actually flushed slightly.

"Not specially. I'm simply stating a fact—And do you mind telling me how old you really are?"

He made a face.

"Thirty-five."

"But that's not *old*, Leigh. It's rather a nice age."

"It's too old for you, my child."

"It's *not* too old, if I don't say so."

"And, being a kind child, you're never going to say so, eh?"

"I might *say* it, if I were in a temper," Nicola admitted frankly, "but I should never really think it."

"Nicola," he said deliberately, "no wonder I'm in love with you."

She glanced at him, still apparently intent on his driving.

"And no wonder," she observed thoughtfully, "that I never had the slightest idea of it. Even now you're talking about it as though it were weather statistics or something equally thrilling."

"How do you expect me to talk of it?"

"Well—" she looked down so that he should not see her eyes were smiling—"Piers, at this point, would undoubtedly kiss me."

With an unmusical grinding of brakes, the car drew to an abrupt standstill at the side of the road, and he turned in his seat so that he was facing her.

"Well, I'm not Piers, you see," he retorted almost savagely. "I'm not given to easy kissing, particularly if I think my kisses would not be welcome."

"What makes you think they wouldn't be?" She hardly knew why she was provoking him. She only knew that she wanted to jerk him out of his habitual self-control and coolness.

"I thought we had this out pretty clearly before we started on our marriage."

"Had *what* out, Leigh? We never even discussed your—your being in love with me," She glanced up in surprise, and as she did so, he leant towards her.

"You little devil," he said quietly, "are you laughing at me?"

"N-not exactly."

He took her in his arms—not roughly, as she had rather expected from his expression, but certainly so that she could not get away easily.

"What do you mean by 'not exactly' I should like to know?"

"Oh, Leigh!—I was just—teasing you a little, and I know I shouldn't and that you take everything terribly seriously and that I'm a frivolous little idiot in some ways, but I'm just human, and sometimes I must——"

"You're not a frivolous little idiot. To me you're the dearest thing in the world. But we've got to have this straight, Nicola. If you want to have our marriage as we arranged, you only have to say so. I love you enough to cut out all the real lovemaking—at least, I think I do," he added in grim parenthesis. "But in that case, there's to be no questioning and teasing. We'll be employer and secretary, who happened to have married because it suits them. I'm not going to have my feelings speared up and examined whenever you want to amuse yourself. If——"

"I wouldn't *do* that," she cried indignantly. "You know I wouldn't. You can't have such a low opinion of me as to think that!"

He put his hand under her chin and turned her face

171

up, peremptorily, as he had that first time he met her.

"Then tell me why you were trying to make me kiss you just now."

"I—don't know. I just——"

"Well, find out, you damned little fool!" he said violently. "Was it to torment me or because you wanted to be kissed? Can't you see how much hangs on it?"

"Leigh!" She was almost more astounded by the fact that he had sworn at her than by anything else which had happened.

"Well, which was it?"

"I don't—"

"If you say you don't know, I think I'll beat you," he said, and from his expression she almost thought he would.

Suddenly she felt most desperately lost and forlorn. In all their relationship he had never been angry like this. She was alone with him—away from the tiresome but safe familiarity of Aunt Katherine's home—utterly and absolutely dependent on Leigh, who was so strangely and unmanageably angry.

In frightened confusion she locked her hands together to keep them from trembling. But with her lips it was a different matter. Those she couldn't keep quite steady. She dropped her eyes, because she was scared to look at him any longer and, as she did so, she felt a subtle difference in the way he was holding her.

It was no longer impossible to escape from his arms. Only he held her with a compelling tenderness rather than by any exertion of strength. She heard him laugh softly, and he kissed her—not the frightening, passionate kiss on her mouth that she had expected, but a gentle, smiling kiss on the side of her cheek.

"My little girl, I'm sorry. You mustn't look like that. I'm behaving abominably—just when I've promised to look after you and care for you. Don't be frightened, darling. I'll never speak to you like that again, and I'll never talk about being so tiresomely fond of you——"

"Oh, Leigh!"

"What, my dear?"

"Only that I want to tell you something." She suddenly put her arms round his neck. "I did want to torment you when I was trying to make you kiss me——"

He interrupted her with a soft laugh, and said:

"Did you, you little wretch? Well, I suppose you're entitled to."

"Oh, no! I wanted to tell you—it's different now. I'm trying to make you kiss me because I want it."

He gave an incoherent little exclamation and kissed her all over her face—her lips and her cheeks; and then he smoothed back her hair and kissed that too. He was smiling now, with no touch of grimness or sarcasm, but with tenderness and amusement and a certain gay confidence which made her realize that he never *had* been quite confident with her before. Peremptory and even dictatorial, but never with that happy confidence which comes only from loving and being loved.

She found she was returning his kisses, eagerly and naturally—for the only reason which mattered—she wanted to. She didn't think any longer about Piers or Aunt Katherine or Miss Pottington or any of the figures that had filled the background of her world until now. She was alone in a sunlit world with Leigh, and everything which had ever happened to her was of no importance except that it had led up to this.

After what seemed a long time, he held her a little away from him and smiled.

"I didn't dare to ask you before. How do you like being married?"

She laughed.

"Love it—in the circumstances." And then, after a moment—"There's something I want to know, Leigh. Did you *really* take advantage of Piers's absence, and quite unscrupulously get everything fixed just because his back was turned?"

Her husband made a slight grimace that was at least half-genuine dismay.

"Oh, lord, am I going to lose all this intoxicating new favour if I confess to that?"

"I shan't stop loving you," Nicola said deliberately, "whatever you tell me."

"*What* was the word you used?" He bent his head down to hers, as though he could hardly believe what he had heard.

"You heard me."

"Did I?" He was smiling. "I thought I must have imagined it—And now you want to know the truth about my scheming. Well then, I *did* use Piers's absence quite deliberately. The moment he turned from the telephone that day, to tell me he had to leave at once on a long tour of inspection, I decided to ask you to marry me. What have you to say to that?"

"That it was very hard on poor Piers."

"Well, my darling, I don't want to say any more against Piers, because somehow, I find at this moment that I wish everyone in the world well—even my graceless young cousin. But I think we're both agreed that he is an incurable philanderer. Just now I'm even willing to believe that it's not entirely his own fault. He has great charm, lots of women have been silly about him, and an unhappy marriage hasn't improved matters. But I didn't intend that he should ruin your happiness, since you were the most precious thing in the world to me—whether you married me or not."

She took his hand in hers and held it tightly.

"I don't think Piers wanted to make me unhappy."

"Oh, he didn't want to, Nicola. He didn't *want* to make anyone unhappy. He wished the whole world well—with the possible exception of me, though I doubt even that. The only thing was that he simply couldn't deny himself anything that he wanted, for such a small reason as someone else's good. Even yours. Do you really think he planned seriously to marry you before this happened?"

Nicola thought of Piers's easy lovemaking, which had never resolved itself into any definite declaration—of his careless confession: "I never plan for the future."

"No," she said honestly. "No, I don't."

"And—equally—do you suppose he would ever have let you marry me, if he had been there from the beginning to argue against it? Why, the affront to his *amour propre* at the idea of my cutting him out would have seemed sufficient reason in itself for his opposing it tooth and nail."

Nicola laughed reluctantly.

"I suppose you're right."

"So, you see, it was my heaven-sent opportunity that he should go away for so long. But I couldn't even wait to try to make you love me first. Miss Pottington and her scandalmongering had to supply the motive.

I could only hope that, somehow, with all the cards stacked against me, I could still make you love me before you decided to claim your divorce."

"Divorce!—Oh, yes, of course. I was going to divorce you later on, wasn't I?"

"You were. Whenever the marriage of convenience had served its purpose."

"Well, it has now, hasn't it?"

"Has what?" He spoke sharply.

"Served its purpose."

"What do you mean?" He actually paled a little.

"It's kept us together long enough to make me realize how I felt. We needn't think about it any more. It's turned into a love-match."

"Oh—" he gave a slight laugh that was half angry, half relieved. "Are you going to spend the rest of your married life administering these vile shocks to me?"

"I'm sorry, darling." She smiled contritely, and at her use of the endearment, his eyes sparkled.

"Very well. And now perhaps we've spent enough time parked at the side of the road. Do you realize that we're on our honeymoon, my darling?—that the world is ours—but that we're many more miles than we should be from the place where we're going to stay?"

"It doesn't matter." Nicola slid comfortably far down in the seat, as he started the car again. "Nothing matters. Not even the fact that Angela has come to live in Longheedon."

"And who the deuce may Angela be?"

Nicola explained. But Leigh seemed hardly more impressed than Diana had been.

"I don't see that she can matter much," he said.

176

"Don't you? Well, she happens to be one of the few people who know it was *Piers* who was there that night."

"The devil! But do you suppose she will remember?"

"The Angelas of this world never forget a face, dear. They make wonderful witnesses in divorce suits."

"Well, that is rather awkward, of course."

They both considered the situation in silence. Then Nicola said:

"I don't care. I'm sick of trying to foresee trouble and guard against it. I'm going to enjoy my honeymoon, and do any worrying afterwards."

He laughed quietly and, taking her hand, put it on the wheel under his.

"Leigh——"

"Yes?"

"Oh—nothing much, I suppose. I'm surprised to find you have such—such lover-like ways."

"Believe me, you're no more surprised than I am," he told her, and they both laughed.

After that, they drove in silence, both busy with their own thoughts, both happier than they had ever been in their lives before.

During the hurried, rather frightening weeks of her engagement, Nicola had hardly thought of her honeymoon at all. Or, if she did, she thought of it with reluctance, as something which had to be lived through, but which could hardly be other than harassing.

That she would be quietly and supremely happy, revelling in the single companionship of a man who had always slightly frightened her, had been quite beyond her imagination. But that was how it was.

177

Not that Leigh changed very much from the man she had always known. He was just as much given to his occasional grimness, to his faintly cynical comments, and to his sarcastic judgments. Only now it didn't matter. She knew that he loved her and that she had nothing to fear from him. She also found that, underneath the rather forbidding exterior, he was essentially kind-hearted and that he was invariably gentle with her if he thought he had distressed her in the least.

The wonderful feeling that one was the dear centre of someone's universe—the feeling she had always had with her father, and so entirely lacked in the bustling, self-sufficient circle of Aunt Katherine's household—was hers once more. It seemed to Nicola that, in stumbling after safety and an escape from censure, she had quite naturally found happiness.

If only, when they got back home, people would leave them alone! ("People" meaning particularly Miss Pottington, of course.) Nicola thought she would have very little more to ask of life if she might just be allowed to enjoy her happiness with Leigh, without scandal and curiosity dogging her.

When she said something of the sort to him one evening, he passed his arm round her and replied:

"But, darling child, we don't even have to go back to Longheedon, if you don't want to. We'll live somewhere else."

"Do you mean—give up Thorpe Compton?"

"If you don't want to live there."

"Oh, but I do, Leigh. And anyway—" Nicola set her mouth— "I won't be driven away from home—*our* home—by a tattling old woman. I've given in quite

enough to scandalmongering and—and bothering what
other people say."

"Even to the extent of marrying someone you
thought you didn't want," he reminded her with a
smile.

"Oh, that! That was just a piece of luck I didn't
quite deserve."

"I think you deserve all the luck in the world," he
said, and dropped a kiss on the top of her head. "But
you're right in wanting to go back and face it out.
Nothing can really hurt us now, and perhaps nothing
further will come out, in any case."

Nicola had considerable doubts about the last suggestion, but she said no more of it, and for the rest of
their honeymoon they were content to enjoy each day
as it came, without worrying over the future.

On the very last morning of all, Nicola received a
letter from home. She recognized it at once as coming
from Diana.

Dear Nic, the letter ran, *I hope you've enjoyed
your honeymoon. Two days after you had gone,
Piers turned up again. He didn't stay at Thorpe
Compton but at the pub in the village. (Mother pre-
fers 'inn', as you know, but it's a pub when all's said
and done.) He seemed inclined to mooch (or is it
'mouch'?) about, looking a bit sorry for himself, so I
suppose he's a bit sore that Leigh got one jump ahead
of him. Anyway, what I meant to tell you was that
Miss Pottington's dear little Angela seems to have
taken a peek at him and run off to tell Miss P. that
he was the man with you that time. It's not my
business, of course, whether it was or not, and I*

179

*don't care anyway, as it's entirely your own affair,
but I thought you'd like to know the latest version,
so that you can decide what you're going to say and
how you're going to say it. Give Leigh a kiss from
me, if it won't embarrass you to do so, and love to
yourself.—Diana.*

Nicola folded up the letter and began to stir her
coffee.

It was too bad! If she had really been living a
questionable life her "past" could hardly have popped
up to confront her so often and so embarrassingly. And
now this story would be particularly hateful for Leigh,
because everyone would think he was the poor deceived husband, devoted to a wife who had really been
carrying on with his own cousin.

On impulse, Nicola thrust the letter into her handbag. She would have to see how she could handle this
herself. She *would not* worry Leigh afresh.

Leigh, to be sure, looked singularly unworried, both
during breakfast and during the long drive home afterwards. But perhaps because of that very fact, she felt
more anxious than ever to keep him serene and un-
troubled.

Thorpe Compton looked beautiful in the evening
sunshine—much more beautiful, now it was her own
home, than it had ever looked when it was simply the
place where her employer lived.

"Leigh, it's lovely coming home."

"Does it really feel like home?—or are you long-
ing to get over to your aunt's place and see them all?"

"Oh, *this* is home! And it feels like it. Of course
Aunt Katherine was always wonderfully good to me—

180

often much more so than I deserved—but her house was *their* home. They'd all been there so many, many years before I ever put in an appearance. Even Edward. It can't be the same as one's own home then."

He didn't answer that, but merely smiled in a satisfied little way, and said:

"All the same, we'll go and see them this evening, eh?"

"Yes, Leigh, I think so. Aunt Katherine would be a bit surprised and hurt if we didn't. Besides, I should like to see Edward and Di."

"Only those two?" He looked amused.

"Oh, well—" she hadn't realized quite how clearly she had shown her preference. "The others aren't much interested in me, you know. I don't know that Di and Edward are exactly *interested*, of course. Only they actively like me, whereas the other three amiably tolerate me. It's rather different."

"No wonder it's nice being loved." He put his arm round her.

"It's wonderful being loved!" Nicola said. And she thought she was hardly afraid even of Miss Pottington after that.

Later that evening, however, she was not so sure.

Leigh and she walked over to Aunt Katherine's house by way of the village, because he wanted to look in and see his bank manager about something. It was quite impossible to protest, of course, but Nicola recalled with acute anxiety that the bank manager's house was not more than fifty yards from Miss Pottington's cottage. And at this time in the evening, when most people were at leisure and inclined to be out enjoying the last of the evening sunshine, Miss Pottington was almost sure to be happily ensconced behind the window-curtains of her sitting-room, observing all that she could, and prepared, at any moment, to whip aside the curtain and tap peremptorily on her window, if she saw any crony of hers go by.

As they entered the main street of the village, Nicola was not particularly reassured to observe the indiscreet Angela, hurrying by on the other side of the road. She cast a furtive glance of interest at Nicola and her escort but, however cordially she had intended the wedding greetings which Miss Pottington had conveyed, she seemed to have changed her attitude now. There was no smile of recognition from her and, indeed, her expression was more sulky than friendly.

Leigh, of course—unaware equally of Angela, the nearness of Miss Pottington's cottage, and the new situation generally—went on talking to Nicola, who replied as best she could, considering that at least half her thoughts were on other things.

As they came abreast of Miss Pottington's cottage, she turned her head the other way. But quite in vain. A frantic tap-tap-tapping broke out upon the window pane as though an agitated woodpecker had suddenly found it had been idle for half an hour and must now make up for lost time.

"Nicola!" screamed Miss Pottington faintly from behind the glass. Then, as she got the window open, the voice wafted across to them with a clearness impossible to ignore. "Nicola! Dear Nicola! Just the person I wanted to see!"

Reluctantly Nicola crossed the road to the little gate, with Leigh following more slowly, divided between amusement and annoyance.

"Dear Nicola, do come in for just a *few* moments. I'm so very anxious to see you." Miss Pottington, half-way out of her window, thrust aside a couple of giant sunflowers, the better to view her victim.

"You go on, Leigh," Nicola said over her shoulder. "I shan't be more than a few minutes. I'll meet you outside the manager's house."

"Sure? Don't you want moral support?" he inquired in a smiling whisper.

"No, thank you," Nicola said, not altogether truthfully. But this time, she felt, she would settle the matter herself.

Miss Pottington was already at the door, drawing back the two bolts and one chain which she considered necessary to keep out any burglars who might choose to wander round Longheedon. And with a little nod to Leigh, Nicola went up the garden path.

"Come in, Nicola!" The door was open at last. "That *was* your husband with you, wasn't it?—He won't come in too?—Has another call to make?—Well, perhaps that's *just as well*, because what I have to say is best said to *you*, I think. It's about that *unfortunate* affair at the inn, dear Nicola!"

"I'm sure it is," dear Nicola said crisply, as she followed Miss Pottington into her sitting-room. "What did you want to say about it, Miss Pottington? I haven't very much time to spare." And she braced herself for whatever was coming.

CHAPTER XIII

"Dear Nicola, I may say that never, in all my life, have I been so *deeply* shocked."

Miss Pottington, while she waved Nicola hospitably to a chair, broke immediately into her story—or, rather, into the near approaches to her story.

"I'm sorry," Nicola said mechanically. "What has shocked you so deeply, Miss Pottington?"

"I'm just *coming* to that," Miss Pottington explained, not altogether accurately. "To begin with, you know— or I think you know—that Angela, my daily, used to work——"

"Yes, I know all about that," Nicola interrupted, feeling unequal to the strain of hearing that part recapitulated.

"Well, as you know, I am always very kindly and, I might almost say motherly, with any girl who is in my employment. At first I let her run on a good deal. But if I had realized the—the terrible *shock* in store for me, I should certainly have silenced her in the beginning."

"Miss Pottington, you're taking rather a long while to lead up to the fact that I've done something which shocked you greatly. Suppose you come to the point." Nicola's nervous anxiety made her speak a little more breathlessly than she had intended.

But the result was not at all what she had expected.

"You, dear Nicola? But you have done nothing to shock me!" Miss Pottington seemed genuinely sur-

184

prised. "It is of Angela that I am talking. My dear, I find that she is the most *arrogant little liar* I have ever come across. These stories—these highly-coloured inventions—are nothing but lies from beginning to end. Imagine, if you can, the *shock* it was to me when I found that she was even telling lies about my own dear brother—I think you met—oh, no you didn't. But anyway, it doesn't matter now. He was with me *that morning*, and I find that this wretched girl actually had the affrontery to tell Mrs. Evans that *my brother* left without paying his bill. My brother, Nicola! One of the most highly-respected men in the whole county of Cumberland!"

Miss Pottington paused with such impressive drama, that Nicola was impelled to murmur:

"How dreadful!"

Really, her thoughts were in a whirl. What on earth had this to do with her?

"But that isn't all, dear Nicola. This wretched girl invented the most ridiculous story about you. She pointed out your husband's *cousin* as the man she would have liked, in her scandalous young mind, to couple with you. You can imagine how severely I reprimanded her for such wicked invention—such defamation of character. I have no idea if she has set this preposterous story about the village, but I felt bound to warn you of it, and of course, my dear, you can *rely on me* to contradict it everywhere."

"Thank you, Miss Pottington," Nicola said in a slightly stunned manner. The discovery of Miss Pottington as the chief champion of her good name was altogether too startling to be accepted in the first moment.

"I am ashamed even to think it now," Miss Pottington ran on, quite untruthfully in any case, "but at first I even wondered if there were something in what the miserable child said. But when I learned that she had been assailing *my brother's* character I understood at once the true worth of her statements. I need hardly tell you, dear Nicola, that the clearing of your name—" all bygones now appeared to be bygones, Nicola noticed— "gave me the *utmost* personal pleasure."

"Thank you," murmured Nicola again, somewhat embarrassed by the palpable untruth of this.

"Not at all, dear. It is a social duty. I felt I had to tell you all about it, just as soon as I saw you. And now I won't keep you any more. I am sure that *someone else* values your company even more than I do."

With an arch smile, Miss Pottington began to usher her still bewildered visitor towards the door.

"You're going up to your dear aunt's house, of course?—My *very* kindest regards to her. And you might tell her that after next week I shall be without a daily, and if she does hear of anyone——"

"Yes, of course. Good-bye, Miss Pottington."

"Good-bye, my dear. *So* pleased to have seen you."

Slightly dazed, Nicola came out into the sunny street once more, to find Leigh waiting a little anxiously for her.

"All right?" He came up to her at once.

"Oh, yes, Leigh!" She laughed rather breathlessly and, slipping her arm into his, she hugged his arm affectionately. "More than all right."

"Really?" He raised his eyebrows amusedly. "What has happened then?"

"Miss Pottington has instituted herself as the chief

champion of my good name."

"But I thought——"

"Yes. So did I. But she's a quick-change artist in these matters. Oh, Leigh, I'm so—so relieved and happy. I'll tell you about it."

As they walked slowly up the hill to Aunt Katherine's house, she described the miraculous change in Miss Pottington's attitude, and they were still laughing about it together, when Edward came puffing up behind them on his bicycle.

"My goodness," he said, as he dismounted. "You two sound as though married life's all right."

"It is," Leigh assured him. While Nicola cried:

"Oh, Edward dear, hello!" with rather more obvious affection than he liked.

"It's a good thing you took my advice, isn't it?" Edward looked at Nicola with owlish benevolence.

"Your advice?"

"About getting married. Don't you remember?—I told you that you'd better."

"Did you really?"

"Yes, of course. That afternoon in the wood-shed. Talk about girls being ungrateful!"

"She's not ungrateful, old chap. She's just too happy to remember anything much at the moment," Leigh explained. "But we won't forget, either of us, that we owe you a debt of gratitude."

"Oh, that's all right." Edward showed slight signs of self-conscious pleasure.

"Not at all," Leigh assured him gravely. "We shall hope to discharge the debt sometime."

Edward looked at him searchingly, to see if that were

a joke. Then, apparently reassured on the seriousness of the point, he said with elaborate casualness:

"Well, you might like to know it's my birthday next month. Now you're in the family, I mean. It's the fourteenth."

Especially for you . . .

A Treasury of
HARLEQUIN ROMANCES
Golden
Harlequin Library

Many of the all-time favorite Harlequin Romance Novels have not been available, until now, since the original printing. But now they are yours in an exquisitely bound, rich gold hardcover with royal blue imprint.

THREE COMPLETE UNABRIDGED NOVELS IN EACH VOLUME.

And the cost is so very low you'll be amazed!

Handsome, Hardcover Library Editions at Paperback Prices! ONLY $2.25 each volume.

Start your collection now. See following pages for brief story outlines.

GOLDEN HARLEQUIN $2.25 PER VOLUME
Each Volume Contains
3 Complete Harlequin Romances

☐ VOLUME 28

CITY OF DREAMS by Elizabeth Hoy   (No. 542)
When Julie arrived excitedly at the lovely Venetian Palazzo,
she found things quite different — not at all as she expected.

DANGEROUS OBSESSION by Jean S. MacLeod   (No. 651)
Faith's fascination for Dr. Maribeau's reputation was so great
that she married him, knowing little of the man himself.

UNTIL WE MET by Anne Weale   (No. 855)
The highly successful star of the Parisian cabaret circuit was
really Joanna Allen who had everything except the one thing
that really mattered.

☐ VOLUME 29

NURSE ELLIOTT'S DIARY by Kate Norway   (No. 525)
Lucy Elliot's diary gives a vivid and endearing picture of her
work and her love, set against an authentic hospital background.

WHERE NO ROADS GO by Essie Summers   (No. 784)
In New Zealand's breathtaking beautiful Fiordland, a young
girl struggles to preserve her newfound love.

WHITE DOCTOR by Celine Conway   (No. 620)
Romance emerges on a Burmese island, while one white doctor and two nurses wage a ceaseless war on tropical disease.

☐ VOLUME 30

CHILD FRIDAY by Sara Seale   (No. 896)
Friday's child is loving and giving, but could Emily give any
hope to the blind, embittered Dane Merritt?

HEART SPECIALIST by Susan Barrie   (No. 587)
Dr. Dauder, a Parisian specialist, was famed for his knowledge
of the human heart — every heart, except his own.

CHILDREN'S NURSE by Kathryn Blair   (No. 633)
Linda's ideas on child care were quite different from the
Marquez de Filano's, and her quiet obstinacy intrigued him.

E

GOLDEN HARLEQUIN $2.25 PER VOLUME
Each Volume Contains
3 Complete Harlequin Romances